His voice

and husky

It sent shivers down Camryn's spine when Patrick said, "Has anyone told you what a beautiful profile you've got?"

He had a knack for doing that, she thought, for giving an ordinary compliment a twist that made it appealing and oh, so seductive to listen to.

How easy it would be to convince myself that he means more than he says. How easy it is to love him—

Above their heads, a skyrocket splintered into green fragments, burst into liquid fire. But the explosion in the sky was no less shattering than the one in Camryn's heart.

I love him. She tried it out hesitantly in her mind, feeling as if she were screaming the words. *I've fallen in love with him. . . .*

Leigh Michaels cannot remember a time when she was not writing—before she was old enough to print, she was dictating to her older sister. She graduated from Drake University at the top of her class, and worked as a newspaper reporter, radio news director, public relations director and research librarian, all of which have provided her with valuable background for her romance novels. She has also taught creative writing at a junior college and has published a textbook on the subject. Her magazine articles have been published in *The Writer*, *Writer's Digest* and other publications. She is married, with two children who have left the nest, leaving her with her photographer husband, a lovable Siamese cat and her faithful mutt Charley. She currently lives in Radar O'Reilly's hometown and enjoys travelling to research her novels.

Books by Leigh Michaels

Don't miss any of our special offers. Write to us at the following address for information on our newest releases.

Harlequin Reader Service
901 Fuhrmann Blvd., P.O. Box 1397, Buffalo, NY 14240
Canadian address: P.O. Box 603,
Fort Erie, Ont. L2A 5X3

A MATTER
OF PRINCIPAL

Leigh Michaels

Harlequin Books

TORONTO • NEW YORK • LONDON
AMSTERDAM • PARIS • SYDNEY • HAMBURG
STOCKHOLM • ATHENS • TOKYO • MILAN

Original hardcover edition published in 1989
by Mills & Boon Limited

ISBN 0-373-03070-3

Harlequin Romance first edition August 1990

CHAPTER ONE

THE first quiet hour of the morning, with a cup of coffee for herself and the delicate scent of vanilla muffins rising from the oven, was always the best part of the day, Camryn thought. This peaceful time of poking about in her kitchen, before the guests started coming downstairs, before the day had a chance to get frantic, was the nicest thing about running a bed and breakfast inn.

But all good and peaceful things ended sooner or later, she told herself philosophically as a buzzer announced that the muffins were done. She pushed her mug aside and hummed as she arranged a china cup and saucer on a lace-lined tray and filled a small pot with freshly brewed coffee.

Camryn nestled two beautifully browned muffins into a napkin-lined basket and added it to the tray, and then stood for a moment, frowning at the arrangement. The strawberries, of course—that was what was missing. There was only one guest at the Stone House for breakfast this morning, but she was going to get the royal treatment.

A movement from the doorway caught her eye as she reached into the refrigerator for the fruit. A small child came quietly into the kitchen, her blonde hair trailing around her shoulders. Cradled in her arms was a black cat, his green eyes half-closed, looking indecently pleased at being carried. The child's feet were bare, and her gingham nightgown ended just below her knees; the sight made Camryn sigh. Susan had grown so much in the last few months that the nightgown just didn't fit right any more, but it was her favourite one, and she absolutely refused to give it up.

'Good morning, Mommy,' the child said, and yawned. Then she saw the tray, and her dark brown eyes turned reproachfully up to meet Camryn's gaze. 'Is that Mrs Ashley's breakfast? Does she have to go home today?'

Camryn dropped a kiss on the soft hair, still disarranged from sleep. 'You'll miss her, won't you, Susan?'

The child nodded.

'Mr Ashley will be released from the hospital today, and they'll fly home this afternoon.' She saw the rebellious quiver of Susan's lower lip, and smothered a sigh.

I'll miss her, too, she wanted to say. If only all of our guests at the Stone House were as pleasant to have around as Mrs Ashley is——

Don't even let yourself think that, Camryn Hastings! she ordered herself. They are all nice people; it's just that some of them are more human than others. . . If you had it to do all over again, you'd make the same decisions and follow the same path, because it was the best way to handle things. And you truly like your job, so don't start feeling sorry for yourself now!

'Would you like to help me take the tray up, Susan, as soon as I finish the strawberries? Put Ipswich outside and wash your hands.'

Susan opened the back door and released the cat, who looked less than pleased at the idea. She stood for an instant on the threshold, and then announced, 'I'll get Mrs Ashley a flower for her tray.'

'Susan—shoes!' But the child was gone, bare feet dancing across the dew-wet lawn to a bed of day-lilies. She came back laughing, two prized blooms clutched in her hand, and thrust them at her mother. 'The grass tickled my toes. I got one for you, too, Mommy. I love you.'

Camryn's heart melted. How could one scold such a child? she thought helplessly. Susan had just turned four, and when a generous impulse struck her she was simply incapable of stopping to think about such mundane things as shoes. Besides, Camryn told herself, it was June. Even though mornings could still be cool and dewy, here on the Wisconsin shore of Lake Michigan, it wasn't as though she had run out into the snow. And she had only been outside for a moment.

They carried Mrs Ashley's breakfast up together, to what had once been the big master bedroom of the Stone House. Now it was the largest of the four guest-rooms, and for the last ten days it had been occupied by Margaret Ashley while she waited for her husband to recuperate from the radical surgery his doctors had recommended. Now he was well enough to travel, so after breakfast Mrs Ashley would finish her packing and go home, and the Stone House would be empty for a day before the next guest came.

It was not very often any more that all the guest-rooms were empty, but it had been a long struggle to build up her business: in the first year that the Stone House had been open, weeks had sometimes gone by between paying guests. It was still a fear that Camryn had to fight now and then. *What if people stopped coming?*

Don't think that way, she told herself. Think that it will be nice to have a break, instead.

Last weekend all the guest-rooms had been full, and the Sunday morning breakfast buffet had been a madhouse. It would be nice to have the house to themselves for a day—just herself and Susan and Ipswich the cat, and of course Sherry Abbott, who rented the tiny apartment on the top floor. . .

How different it all was from what she had planned on the day she had first seen the Stone House. Camryn looked thoughtfully out across the wide landing and down the stairs to where sunshine streamed through the bevelled glass front door and poured itself into gleaming pools on the parquet floor. There was an odd prickle just behind her eyelids. She blinked it away, a little irritated with herself. She seldom cried any more. It had, after all, been a long time ago.

Mrs Ashley opened the door. She was putting the last pin in the knot of white hair at the back of her neck, and she took one look at the tray and shook her head fondly. 'You spoil me, Camryn, dear. Breakfast in bed——

'But I'm too late. You're already dressed.'

'Yes—I'm anxious to get to the hospital today.' She sounded a bit sheepish. 'It sounds foolish, doesn't it—to be afraid that if I'm late the doctors will decide to keep Richard another day? You didn't bring a cup for yourself?'

Camryn carried the tray across to the small, round table in the bay window at the front of the house. 'I have to get Susan ready for nursery school.' She caught a rebellious sparkle in the child's big brown eyes and added, without looking directly at Susan, 'She only goes once a week in the summer, and they do very special things. They're visiting the fire station today.'

Susan looked thoughtfully at the oak floor, where she was drawing lines with her big toe, as if mulling over a giant decision.

Camryn said gently, 'It's time to say goodbye, Susan. I laid your clothes out, but you have to start getting dressed now.'

Susan stuck her lower lip out.

Mrs Ashley gave the child a hug. 'I'm going to miss you both. Camryn, you don't know what a help it's been to me to have you and Susan and this lovely room. With all the uncertainty about Richard's health, and whether he'd even make it through the surgery—well, I think I would have been a screaming wreck if I'd had to go back to an empty hotel room every night, with no one to care how I was feeling.'

'It's been our pleasure.'

'No—it's more than that. I'm going to write to the hospital and suggest that they recommend the Stone House often.'

Camryn managed an emotional thanks; that sort of referral was the kind of advertising that couldn't be purchased at any price, and she wasn't about to turn down guests from any source.

By the time she returned from taking Susan to nursery school, Mrs Ashley's rental car was gone. In the kitchen, Sherry Abbott was wiping up the remains of Susan's breakfast from the top of the centre island. 'What was the child doing to this poor muffin?' Sherry asked. 'Taking it apart molecule by molecule?'

'Something like that.' Camryn poured herself a cup of coffee. 'Fifteen minutes, and then I'll go tackle the cleaning. The whole place needs a polishing——'

'I thought you were going to the bank this morning about your mortgage.'

'I did it yesterday. It was only a matter of a little paperwork to get the loan renewed.'

'I thought once you had a mortgage you always had it—you know, till death us do part.' Sherry darted a look across the table and said, 'Sorry.'

Camryn forced herself to smile. 'Some mortgages last

even longer than that, actually. Oh, Sherry, for heaven's sake, Mitch has been dead for almost four years. I don't whisper the word any more, and you don't need to, either. Sometimes I go days without thinking about him——'

'And sometimes not,' Sherry finished. 'Mostly not. You don't fool me for a minute, Camryn Hastings. You won't even try to meet men——'

'I have no time.'

'And no desire. You're a lovely widow, my dear——'

'Have a muffin, Sherry.'

Sherry sighed and took one. 'All right, you don't have to hit me with a plank; I know the subject is closed. Do you want me to pick Susan up from school? I've got a class at ten, so it's not out of my way at all.' She reached for the butter-dish.

Camryn laughed. 'You're horribly transparent, you know. You'd rather do that than help clean.'

'I certainly would.'

'You did more than your share over the weekend, and we don't have another guest coming in till tomorrow. I've got plenty of time to get things back in shape. Take the day off—go lie in the park and read Proust, or something.'

Sherry wrinkled her nose. 'Do you mind if I make it D H Lawrence instead? That might get some masculine attention.' She picked up her books and a couple of muffins. 'If I find two likely candidates, I'll use muffin crumbs to entice them to follow me home for dinner.' She was gone before Camryn could throw something at her.

Irrepressible Sherry, Camryn thought as she straightened up the kitchen. 'She's like a bottle of champagne,' she told the black cat, who had curled himself carefully around a pot of chives on the window-sill and was lazily watching as she got the cleaning supplies out. 'Full of bubbles, the life of the party, and capable of exploding in any direction. While I——'

While I, she thought, am a can of ginger ale that's been sitting open on the refrigerator shelf too long. The fizz is gone. . .

And that surely shouldn't surprise anyone, not even Sherry. After all, Camryn had been just short of her twenty-second birthday, with a six-month-old baby, when Mitch had died. If it hadn't been for Susan—that tiny scrap of uncomprehending humanity who needed her so desperately—Camryn didn't know what would have happened to her.

'Enough,' she said firmly. 'There is no sense in dwelling on it. You've got Susan, and you've got the Stone House, and you're making a new life for yourself. And the fact that Sherry thinks you need a man to make your life complete is beside the point.'

No, she decided as she carried the vacuum cleaner up the broad staircase, she wasn't going to spend her life waiting around to see if another man turned up. She had herself to depend on now, and that was all she needed. Not that Mitch had been undependable; far from it. But sometimes fate had a way of interfering in the best-made plans. . .

Camryn didn't hear the telephone until she turned the vacuum cleaner off in the front bedroom, but she thought it must have been ringing for a long while; it had that particularly desperate, long-suffering sound.

It was a masculine voice that asked for Mrs Hastings— a nice voice, she thought, mature but still young. It was always fun to predict what her guests would look like and then compare her vision to the reality when they arrived. This one was easy; in his thirties, she'd guess. Perhaps he was arranging a weekend getaway for himself and his wife—a couple of days without the kids. She closed her eyes and tried to remember the reservation schedule posted on her desk down in the breakfast room.

'I'd like to speak to Mrs Hastings, please.' The repetition was crisp.

A professional man, she thought, one with some power—there was a note in his voice that warned he was used to giving orders. She admitted that she was Mrs Hastings.

'I'm Patrick McKenna from Lakemont National Bank. I have your application for a mortgate in front of me, and——'

There was a fragment of disappointment deep inside her. It would have been rather fun to see if she'd been right about his age, and his personality. And the wife and kids, she added, poking fun at herself. This habit of analysing people's voices was getting out of hand!

'A mortgage renewal, you mean, surely?' she corrected briskly. 'The mortgage itself was arranged four years ago——'

'Yes, I know. I've got your files here, Mrs Hastings.'

'Well, it's very simple. It was explained to us at the time, Mr. . .McKenna, did you say? It's a balloon mortgage, which simply means that I have to go through the formality of renewing it every four years——'

That crisp voice cut across her protest. 'What a balloon mortgage means, Mrs Hastings, is that the entire balance of your loan is due within sixty days.'

Camryn's hand clenched the stair railing. 'But that's just not possible,' she whispered.

'Unless a new mortgage is written.'

Camryn started breathing again. 'Well, then, why

don't you get busy and write me one?' she said pleasantly. 'That's what loan officers are for—not scaring honest customers to death!'

'Sometimes they also have to ask tough questions, Mrs Hastings—such as the little related matter of why your mortgage payment hasn't been made yet this month. It was due last week, if you recall.'

'The water-heater broke down, and——'

'I'm afraid that's really not an adequate excuse.'

'Obviously you have no idea of what it costs to replace a water-heater. At any rate, I called the bank and explained that I'd be late——'

'And who did you speak to?'

Camryn shifted her grip on the telephone. 'I can't remember,' she admitted. 'I had no idea I'd need to know her name.'

There was a brief silence, and then a sigh. 'I think we need to talk this over before I can proceed. Can you come into the bank today, Mrs Hastings?'

'I was there yesterday.'

'So I was told. I'm sorry that I wasn't here to assist you, but unfortunately, as things stand, I can't do much to help you.' It was pleasant enough, but absolutely inflexible. 'Shall I expect you today?'

She swore under her breath and thought about putting him off. Today wasn't exactly convenient, with the mess she'd left in the front bedroom, and nothing done yet to the master suite. . .

Don't be a fool, Camryn, she told herself. The sooner you set this madman straight, the better! 'I suppose I can rearrange my schedule. I'm sure you can give me a minute or two to get there.'

The sarcasm seemed to bounce off him. 'I'll be looking forward to our meeting, Mrs Hastings.'

Camryn slammed the telephone down. 'That makes two of us, Mr McKenna,' she growled. 'And after I deal with you, it will be sheer pleasure to talk to your boss!'

It was closer to a half-hour before she pulled open the heavy glass door of the main office of Lakemont National Bank and stalked across the marble lobby to the long row of hushed offices at the back of the building. She'd decided that the interview would be a lot more devastating to an upstart loan officer if she was dressed in something other than the sweat pants and T-shirt she'd been wearing to clean the house. She was still breathing hard from the sheer speed of her change, but she was wearing a trim camel-coloured suit and heels; she'd put on a touch of make-up, and she'd taken out her frustration on her hair, which gleamed like golden-brown honey from the furious brushing it had received.

She took a deep breath and reminded herself that losing her temper would do her no good; the way to handle this was with a tone of sweet reasonableness. It was the kind of thing Mitch had been wonderful at doing. If Mitch was still here, she thought, you wouldn't know what hit you, Mr McKenna!

She almost stumbled on the edge of the deep carpeting that marked the line between the public lobby and the élite offices. She caught herself and bit her lip. For an instant, the pain had been almost too much—the pain of missing Mitch. He had always been the one who took care of this sort of thing. . .

The secretary who had helped her fill out the papers the day before looked up from her typewriter with a look that reminded Camryn of a fear-paralysed rabbit. 'Mr McKenna is expecting you.'

She thought, So he's the sort who terrifies the secretaries in his spare time!

The secretary tapped on a closed door. The plaque on the rich wood surface announced discreetly that Patrick McKenna was a vice-president. Camryn smiled a little and wondered what he'd thought when she had called him a mere loan officer. Well, he would fall a bit harder by the time she was finished, that was all. The title didn't mean much, really; when it came to banks, vice-presidents were a dime a dozen.

His office was not large, but it was well furnished. Three walls were panelled in warm, rich oak; the fourth looked out over the lobby area and was glass, covered with an open-weave, nubby drapery in a soft blue. On the wall behind his desk was a very attractive seascape where waves beat themselves into a rich foam against a rocky shoreline. Standing on a credenza against the side wall was a delicate bronze sculpture of a small child skipping.

The room was quiet, too—so quiet that the sound of the door closing behind the secretary seemed like the clanging of a prison cell's bars. Camryn jumped and then turned, trying to steady her nerves, to face the man standing behind the desk.

Conservative—that was the only word for him, she thought. He was wearing the banker's standard navy pin-striped three-piece suit, a sober dark red tie, a shirt so white it almost had a blue sheen. She couldn't see his feet, but she'd have placed a bet that he was wearing hand-made shoes and black socks. And probably, she thought wildly, plain white boxer shorts as well—there could be no *risqué* polka dots for a man in his position. . .

And yet—his almost black hair was neatly trimmed, but there was a rebellious sort of wave to it. And surely no bank dress-code written since the turn of the century would have approved the heavy gold watch-chain that gleamed against his waistcoat? And his eyes—they were dark blue, and fringed with the most outlandishly long black lashes she'd ever seen. Bedroom eyes, if she'd ever seen a pair. . .

At the moment, however, they were gleaming with something that could only be irritation.

I've wasted his precious time, she thought. Well, isn't that just too bad? She put her chin up and said, without a hint of conciliation, 'I'm so sorry to have kept you waiting.'

Patrick McKenna extended his hand. His handshake was firm and warm and solid. 'Please sit down, Mrs Hastings.'

I was right, she thought illogically. He's just barely into his thirties. That's too young to be a tyrant, but obviously he's got an early start. And no sense of humour, to boot.

She sat down. 'Let's make this fast, shall we, Mr McKenna? I have to pick my daughter up at nursery school in an hour.'

'I'm as anxious as you are to get this straightened out.'

Camryn fought down a twinge of aggravation. He didn't need to be so obvious about it!

'I found the teller you talked to last week, by the way.'

'Thank you,' Camryn said stiffly. 'I'm glad to know that my honesty isn't under suspicion any more.'

He looked at her for a long moment, almost without expression, and flipped open the folder that lay on the polished desk. 'We'll take up the matter of the late payment in a minute. But first I think I should explain to you why we've got this problem now. You don't seem to understand the terms of your existing mortgate.'

'I didn't know there was anything to understand. We decided on the house, we filled out the paperwork, we got the loan, we started paying the money back. Very simple. I don't recall the name of the man who helped us——'

'The gentleman in charge of mortgage lending retired about two years ago, when Lakemont National was purchased by the Logan Banks.'

'I do remember hearing about the buy-out, thank you,' Camryn said crisply.

'What you don't seem to remember was that there was apparently considerable doubt about your financial solidarity at the time you and your husband applied for a mortgage.'

She frowned.

'The fact that you couldn't qualify for a regular mortgage indicates that you didn't have a lot going for you,' he pointed out.

'I suppose that's true,' Camryn said reluctantly. 'Mitch was just finishing his residency at the time, and getting ready to go into practice——'

'As a heart specialist.' When she looked up at him in surprise, he added, 'It's in your application.'

Camryn nodded. 'But——'

'And you weren't working?'

'I had a job, but I was on maternity leave just then.'

He nodded. 'I think I see what happened. A young doctor, without much cash but with a promising future——'

'We had a down payment,' Camryn pointed out. 'Mitch's father had left him some stock, and we sold it.'

'I see. The bank didn't want to offend what would probably be a wonderful customer in the future. At the same time, they didn't feel justified in tying themselves up for thirty years, in case the doctor's promise didn't pay out. So the balloon looked like a good option—four years that way, then if everything still looked good and the practice was holding up, they'd switch to a normal mortgage. If in the meantime Dr Hastings decided to practise meditation instead of medicine, the bank could just decline to write a new mortgage.'

It made a lot of sense, from the bank's point of view. It also left a sick feeling in the pit of Camryn's stomach. 'Self-protection,' she said drily. 'Somehow the bank seems to have taken care of its own interests at the expense of ours.'

Patrick McKenna leaned back in his chair and looked at her steadily. 'It must have been explained to you, Mrs Hastings.'

'I suppose it was, but. . .' She shook her head uncertainly.

'You signed the papers. It's all perfectly legal.'

Camryn knew he was right; it was all laid out there with her signature neatly at the bottom. 'Mitch took care of all of that, you see,' she said. 'I just—signed.' And I already know it wasn't very smart, she thought, so if you have the gall to tell me I was an idiot, Mr McKenna, I'm going to strangle you with your own watch-chain!

He didn't. 'That's all beside the point, now. I'm very sorry that this mess happened, Mrs Hastings; it was careless of my predecessor, and that's one of the reasons Lakemont National isn't an independent bank any more. As it stands, however, the final payment on your balloon is due in sixty days——'

'And that really means that I have to come up with the rest of the money by then?' It was calm, as if it didn't matter to her in the least when the balance came due. And it doesn't make any difference, Camryn thought.

Tomorrow, sixty days, next year—it wouldn't change a thing.

He nodded. 'That's why the timing on your late payment could hardly have been worse. It makes you look irresponsible, and it certainly complicates writing a new mortgage to take the balloon's place.'

'But it doesn't make it impossible?'

For the first time, he smiled. It was a boyish, charming smile, with white teeth gleaming. The skin at the corner of his eyes wrinkled pleasantly, and the eyes themselves held a sort of inward sparkle. 'I think we can manage to work it out. But no more late payments, all right? The problem at the moment is that when you filled out the papers yesterday we didn't get a lot of the necessary information.' He picked up a form from the folder in front of him and frowned at it.

Camryn recognised the neat, precise handwriting as her own. She could almost recite what was on that piece of paper.

'You've included only information about your own assets, and your own business—you're operating a bed and breakfast in the house? You didn't mention that in the original application.'

'I didn't know I was going to be running one.'

Patrick McKenna reached into a desk-drawer and pulled out a sheaf of forms. 'I think it will be easier if we start from scratch,' he said, and picked up a gold pen. 'A lot of this I can fill in later, from the original application, but I'll need to know about Dr Hastings' practice first—things like what his annual income is and what——'

She swallowed hard. 'I don't think you quite understand, Mr KcKenna. My husband is dead.'

If she had ripped the plaque off his office door and hit

him with it, he would probably not have looked quite so stunned.

'Mitch was killed in the crash of a small plane just a few months after we bought the house,' she added softly.

He put down his pen. 'And you've taken over this responsibility ever since? No one has questioned it?'

'Do you think I tried to pull something over on the bank?' Her voice was sharp. 'I didn't. There was certainly no secret about Mitch's death, Mr McKenna. It was on the front page of the newspaper——'

'No, no. That's not what I meant. But surely you considered your options——?'

'What options? If I'd stopped making payments, I'd have lost my home, to say nothing of the money we'd already put into it.'

'You could have sold it.'

'And then where would I have lived? What would I have used for money?'

'There are apartments, Mrs Hastings. And jobs. A house that size is a fantastic drain on your resources.'

'Exactly. So I looked around for what I could do— how I could make it pay for itself—and I started the bed and breakfast. And it's doing very well, thank you.'

'Except for the water-heater,' he said drily. 'Surely the sheer expense is driving you out of business? You'd be better off to rid yourself of this albatross——'

'I'm not trained for anything, Mr KcKenna. I have a daughter to support. Have you ever tried to pay for child care out of the kind of salary a secretary makes? No, of course you haven't.' She waved a dismissing hand at the quiet elegance of the office. 'Believe me, this was the best option I had. I'm at home with my daughter, and I make a living. It's nothing grand, but we have what we need. And I don't plan to let some sanctimonious banker talk me out of doing what I know is right for me. You've got all the information you need to make a decision, right there.'

He looked down at the forms, and then back at her. There was astonishment in his eyes. 'Do you seriously want me to consider your loan application for this size of mortgage based on this information?'

'Yes, I do.'

He said, not unkindly. 'It's going to be turned down, you know. We have rules, and guidelines, and we can't just throw them out the window. You're spending more than half of your income on this house, Mrs Hastings——'

'Yes, I am.' She swallowed hard. 'But remember, please, before you turn me down, that it hasn't been Mitch who's made the payments on that mortgage for almost four years. It's me. Out of my income, inadequate as you seem to think it is. And I've only missed one payment.'

He flipped a page over and looked up at her. 'You missed two within the first year of the loan.'

She thought it over. 'All right, two. But I was just getting started. You know how tough it is with a new business——'

'The business isn't new any more,' he reminded. 'And you've missed a third payment, now.'

'This one is different. It isn't missing, it's late. And it's just bad luck that I've got this cash-flow problem right now——'

'But how often is it going to happen in the future?' He sounded a little sad, but determined, and laid the papers aside. 'Mrs Hastings, my conscience will simply not let me recommend approval of this loan. . .'

His conscience? she thought. And what about my

conscience? My debt to my daughter—to raise her as her father would have wanted? Mitch's daughter will not be raised by baby-sitters. She will not be a latch-key child.

'And the risk to the bank, Mr McKenna?'she said crisply. 'Are you certain that isn't the reason your conscience is paining you?'

'That, too,' he admitted. 'I don't understand how you've been doing it, and I can't be a part of letting it go on.'

Her gaze came to rest on the bronze sculpture. Whoever had chosen the bank's art collection, Camryn thought, had done so to good effect. How could anyone with the statue of a child in his office be accused of putting mere mercenary concerns in front of humanitarian ones?

She stood up, because if she stayed in his office five more minutes she knew she would do something she would regret forever. 'I'm only asking for a fair appraisal, Mr McKenna,' she said crisply. 'Look over my application. Come and see the Stone House. And then do whatever your conscience dictates—if you really have one.'

CHAPTER TWO

PATRICK MCKENNA was on his feet. 'Mrs Hastings, I——'

'I'm sure I can trust you to call me if you need any further information.' The flared skirt of her camel suit swirled as she turned towards the door, displaying slender legs. 'And you'll let me know when you've made a decision, of course.' It was not a question.

'The matter is not entirely in my hands, you understand.'

She stopped and turned to look at him, her hand on the knob of the half-open door. 'Mr McKenna,' she chided. 'I'm shocked. You didn't seem the sort who would pass the blame for your unpopular decisions on to someone else.' She tossed her head and her glossy brown hair shimmered under the strong office lights as the strands settled back into place against her shoulders.

In the reception area, the secretary raised her head from her ledger book with astonishment. Next to her desk, in an upholstered chair, a young blonde woman looked up from a magazine and inspected Camryn from head to toe. 'Goodness,' she murmured. 'I'm glad I waited for you, Patrick. You must be perishing for lunch and some civilised company.' She stood up slowly. She was six inches taller than Camryn, and there was elegance in every line of her tall, slim body, in every graceful movement she made.

His wife? Fiancée? Not co-worker, Camryn would bet; she doubted any mere bank employee could afford that label. If that dress hadn't come from a name designer, she thought, she'd slice everything in her own wardrobe into ribbons!

The blonde slipped a slender hand into the crook of Patrick McKenna's elbow. 'We'll go to Brannigan's, I think,' she said. Her smooth, sultry voice was only a murmur, and yet Camryn knew she was intended to hear it. 'And we'll have a nice drink, and we won't talk about nasty things like business.' Her eyes flicked over Camryn, and then turned admiringly to her companion. She was precisely the same height as he was.

Camryn told herself briskly that she didn't have time to be upset because of a glitzy blonde's catty remarks; she was already late to pick up Susan. It didn't help much. The shock of what Patrick McKenna had told her was still sinking in as she crossed the lobby and went out to her car, and that was much more stunning than anything the blonde girl could have said. There was a hopeless, helpless feeling deep inside her, like a boulder in the pit of her stomach. Was she really going to lose her home? Her precious, beloved Stone House. . .?

She wanted to cry. No, she wanted to go back and shake Patrick McKenna by the hair until he guaranteed that she would get the loan she had to have.

Susan was waiting for her. The child was scarcely belted into the front seat of the car before she began bubbling over with stories about her visit to the fire station. She rattled cheerfully for several minutes, and then stopped abruptly. 'Mommy, you're not listening,' she accused.

Camryn forced herself to smile. 'Sorry, darling. I was thinking about something else, that's all.' She stopped the car under the porte-cochère behind the house and looked up at the stone carvings beside the back door.

Lunch at Brannigan's, she thought. He'd probably sip his vodka and tonic—scratch that, she decided; with a name like Patrick McKenna, Irish whiskey was no doubt his drink—and tell his charming companion all about the tough morning he'd had, and the unreasonable Mrs Hastings. And then he'd go back to the bank and shuffle papers for an hour or two, to make her believe he had really considered it, and then he would call to tell her how sorry he was that he couldn't recommend her loan. . .

'Susan, let's pack a picnic and go to the park, shall we? I don't have to work this afternoon.'

And I don't want to be home, she thought. Perhaps in the fresh air I won't even have to think about it for a little while. He can't force me to give up my house, can he? Even if Lakemont National won't give me a mortgage, there are other banks. Surely there is a banker somewhere in this city who has a little vision, who wants to encourage free enterprise, small business, and the American dream of a mother staying at home to raise her child?

You're beginning to sound as if you're running for office, she told herself drily. She changed into shorts and running shoes and a T-shirt, and tossed their lunch into a bag. There was one good thing about picnics, she thought. To a four-year-old, anything that came out of a brown paper bag in the park tasted a great deal better than it did on a plate at home.

She played with Susan for most of the afternoon, pushing her swing, joining her on the helter-skelter, running and laughing and romping as if she were a child herself. And this, she thought as she pulled up at the edge of the sandbox in a dead heat with her giggling daughter, is what Mr KcKenna thinks I should give up.

Get rid of the house, go back to a regular job, put Susan in day care—that's the sensible thing to do. Well, she thought rebelliously, he wouldn't think it was so sensible if it was him, or his child.

Not that he was likely to ever face such a situation. The glitzy blonde would probably hire a full-time nanny so she wouldn't ever have to miss out on lunch at Brannigan's. . .

It wasn't that Camryn thought day-care was such a dreadful fate for a child, actually. But there were so many children, and so few really good day-care centres. And even if she found a good one she would have trouble paying for the service. It had been one thing to work at low-paying secretarial jobs when she was first married; Mitch had been working, too, when he could fit a job around the demands of medical school, and they'd lived in student housing. With her minuscule wages, they'd been able to keep things going. But they hadn't had Susan then. . .and they hadn't intended for Camryn to work forever.

So much for my good resolutions not to dwell on the problem, she thought ruefully as they walked home at mid-afternoon. Susan's feet were dragging, and now and then she yawned. Camryn was beginning to think of the mess she'd left in the front bedroom. Damn Patrick McKenna, anyway!

As they turned the corner on to Kenosha Street the sight of the big cut-stone house, its red-tile roof glimmering in the warm sunlight, caught at her heart. Give it up, after she had worked so hard to keep it going?

'Never,' she said between her teeth. 'There will be a way. There has to be a way. . .'

There was a car in the driveway of the Stone House, a small silver Mercedes convertible with the top down.

Camryn ran through her mental list of friends and concluded that she no longer knew anyone who could afford to drive that sort of car. And since she wasn't expecting a guest, she didn't bother to hurry her footsteps. Any door-to-door salesman who was driving that car was selling something she couldn't afford, anyway!

As she and Susan came up the path hand in hand, Patrick McKenna turned from the front door and walked briskly across the wide porch to the steps. He stopped abruptly on the top step and looked down at them.

'No wonder you didn't answer the door,' he said lightly. He'd pushed his jacket back, and his hands rested lightly on trim hips. His hair wasn't even mussed, despite the convertible.

Perhaps, Camryn thought, banking pays better than I thought.

She hated to think what she looked like herself, after an afternoon in the park. Hot and sweaty and dusty, with her shorts crumpled and her hair wind-blown—he couldn't have chosen a worse time.

'If I'd known you were coming to call, I'd have had the kettle boiling.' Camryn fished her key out of her shoe and unlocked the big door.

'You did invite me to come and see the Stone House.'

'Frankly, I didn't expect that you'd do it—certainly not so promptly.'

'I thought you'd appreciate getting it out of the way before the weekend.'

'Don't you have any other customers to look after?' Why didn't I come straight home this afternoon? she berated herself. The place looks as if it hasn't been cleaned in a year. Hope, however, was beginning to dawn in her heart. He'd had an opportunity to review her files, to confirm that she'd made her payments as faithfully—almost as faithfully, she reminded herself—as any bank could wish. Surely——?

'We didn't part on the most friendly of terms this morning,' he reminded. 'I thought if we could finish our discussion, perhaps you would better understand the bank's position.'

Camryn's heart dropped a bit. That didn't sound promising. She felt a tug on her hand as Susan leaned around her to inspect Patrick McKenna. It was a bit odd, she thought. This warm-hearted and happy child was never shy at meeting the strangers who came to the Stone House. Usually she bounced right up and introduced heself. This time she was practically trying to hide.

It just proves, she thought, that children have wonderful instincts. Sharks, wild dogs, and bankers—Susan has an inborn fear of all three. . .

'Whatever you like, Mr McKenna,' she said, and led the way into the big entrance hall.

In mid-afternoon the hall was always in soft shadow, except for the sunlight that spilled down the stairs from the solarium that opened off the first landing. The solarium, with its white wicker furniture and green plants and its view of the garden below was normally Camryn's favourite room, but it was also Susan's play area, and she hadn't got that far with her cleaning this morning. So she led Patrick McKenna into the formal living-room instead.

'If you wouldn't mind waiting a minute while I settle Susan for her nap,' she began. He nodded, and she hurried up the stairs to the child's top-floor bedroom. Susan was so worn out that she went down without protest, and was asleep almost before her mother left the room. While the coffee perked Camryn arranged a neat tray, and after a moment's consideration added a basket of muffins. It couldn't hurt to give him something to do with his hands, she thought, and if he was eating she might even get the chance to have her say. . .

He was standing at the far end of the living-room when she came in with the coffee, and she would have sworn he was reading the titles on the built-in book-shelves that filled the wall. But he showed no sign of embarrassment as he came to help her with the tray, and she concluded that he must have been simply looking out of the window instead. Too bad it wasn't a little later in the season, she thought. The autumn flowers were going to be outstanding this year. . .

Don't be foolish, she told herself. He's not the average guest who might be persuaded to recommend the Stone House to his friends. The flowers wouldn't matter a damn to him. You're fighting for your life here, Camryn—don't forget it.

She poured his coffee and said, with a weak attempt at humour, 'I don't suppose you came to tell me that the bank will be happy to give me the loan.'

'No, I'm afraid I didn't. Mrs Hastings, are you absolutely certain about not selling the house? It's worth more than it was when you bought it——'

'Cream and sugar?'

'No, thank you.' The china cup looked fragile in his hand. 'You'd have a small nest-egg left to invest——'

'Would it be enough to live on?' she asked calmly.

'Of course not. But——'

'Please don't forget that it isn't just a matter of selling the house,' she pointed out. 'It would mean giving up my business—the way I make my living.' She shook her head. 'I'm staying here.'

'You know that it's unrealistic to think you can handle that sort of debt—don't you?'

'But I already am handling it.'

'By straining your income past the limits. When the loan was made, your husband estimated that he would be making at least ten times what you're taking in now——'

'Isn't it up to me how I spend my money? If I want to put most of it into my business——'

'What if you get sick and can't do the heavy work this sort of business requires?'

She looked at him for a long moment and mused, 'You're a rare man, Mr McKenna—most males still think cleaning the house means lifting nothing heavier than a duster.'

'You haven't answered the question.'

Obviously, she thought, flattery isn't going to get me anywhere. 'I've got some household help. I rent the big bedroom on the top floor as sort of a self-contained apartment, in return for a hand with the cleaning when I've got every room full.'

'What if the guests stop coming, Mrs Hastings?'

'Can't you ask that kind of question about any small business? That doesn't make it likely to happen. Oh, be reasonable, Mr McKenna. I can go to another bank, you know——'

'I almost wish you would. Then you might at least admit that I'm being as reasonable as I can. Do you have any assets that aren't listed on that application? If you could pay off part of the balance, so you wouldn't need such a large loan——'

Camryn shook her head. 'If you're asking if I have some dusty stock certificates tucked away in a shoe box somewhere—no, I don't. I don't have any gold bars hidden under my bed, either. But doesn't my character count for anything at all?' She sipped her coffee. 'I know you don't have to say it. You're thinking that I'm quite a character, all right.'

A muscle twitched beside his mouth, and for an instant there was a gleam of humour in those dark blue eyes. Then it was sternly repressed. 'You said earlier today that you have no skills. Surely there is something that you can do?'

'Yes, there is.' She broke a vanilla muffin and buttered it, and then looked up at him. 'I'm really very good at running a bed and breakfast. You should try these, they're wonderful, if I do say so myself.'

The black cat jumped up on the couch beside Camryn and eyed the muffin covetously.

'See?' She fed the animal a morsel. 'Ipswich even guarantees them. Which is one more reason I want to stay in the house—I'd have enough trouble finding an apartment I can afford without worrying about whether Susan can keep her cat there.'

He didn't even argue that one. Instead he reached for a muffin. 'Didn't your husband have life insurance?'

'Some, but most of the money went to paying off his medical school debts. I invested what was left in the bed and breakfast to get started.'

'I'm beginning to wonder why the bank let him borrow anything at all,' Patrick McKenna grumbled. 'They should at least have demanded that he buy insurance to cover his debt. And didn't it ever occur to him that you might need an income?'

Her voice was suddenly like a steel thread. 'If you're implying that Mitch was careless of my well-being, let me assure you that he certainly didn't intend to leave me in this situation. In any case, it's too late to argue about what Mitch could or should have done. If you take my house away from me, I don't know what else Susan and I can do. From a purely financial standpoint, I'd be better off to go on welfare than to struggle to make ends meet on the sort of job I can get.'

He jumped up and paced across the room. 'Anybody who could qualify for welfare has no business applying for a mortgage!'

Camryn leaned forward, her hands clasped. Her voice was low and passionate. 'So why don't you help keep me out of the system? Surely there is some way you can justify giving me a chance——?'

'Mrs Hastings, bankers get fired for making crazy loans. You have no reserves, nothing to carry you over a difficult period. An illness or a sudden drop in occupancy rates and you'd be done. If I made this loan, my job would be on the line.'

'Well, if you don't, my life is.' She leaned back against the couch, her eyes closed. She was suddenly exhausted, drained of every trickle of energy. What was the use of trying to persuade him? She wished that he would just go away, before she started to cry. 'The whole idea of banking is very simple, isn't it? You won't loan me the money unless I can prove that I really don't need it at all.'

'Please don't be sarcastic, Mrs Hastings. Banks have rules—for good reason, too. Let's take it again, from the top. Is there anyone in your family who might loan you some money? If you only weren't delinquent, it would help.'

Camryn didn't bother to open her eyes. 'Do you think I haven't already considered obvious things like that? My mother lives in Arkansas on an inadequate annuity left to her by my father; my only brother teaches algebra in an inner-city school in Chicago. And I have no aunts and uncles—rich or otherwise.'

'I'm sorry I asked.' He sighed, and added quietly, 'The damnable thing is that when I listen to you explain why you want to stay here, it makes sense—despite all the rules.'

She opened one eye warily, and stared at him. He sounded as if he meant it.

'If there is anything that would allow an exception. . .' He sounded dissatisfied, as if he was grasping at straws, but Camryn wasn't about to ask uncomfortable questions. 'Perhaps if I reviewed your bookkeeping records it would give me some ideas.'

She cleared her throat and said, 'Absolutely.' It was a husky, mellow whisper. 'You can see anything you want.'

He smiled at her then, and in the dark blue eyes a lively flame of amusement danced. 'Be careful how you say that,' he murmured. 'I might conclude that you're trying to bribe me.'

Camryn felt a deep, horrified flush start at the neckline of her T-shirt and rise till her whole face was a sheet of embarrassed colour. 'That was the farthest thing from my mind,' she began stiffly. 'I certainly did not intend——'

The doorbell pealed, its rich, mellow tones ringing through the rooms. Gratefully, Camryn jumped up, dumping Ipswich out of her lap, and went to answer it.

On the porch, a woman was waiting, tapping her toes on the welcome mat. She was probably in her late fifties. Her lavender dress and matching coat were well cut, but not particularly suited to her angular figure and sharp features. Behind her a much younger man stood, with his hands in his pockets. He was shifting nervously from one foot to the other, and as soon as Camryn opened the door he stepped forward. 'Mrs Hastings? I'm John Marlow—I reserved a room for my mother for the weekend.'

Camryn opened her mouth to say, 'Yes, you did—starting tomorrow!' Then she realised that, though she had never seen the young man before, he looked familiar, and she remembered that she had seen the same pleading look on her daughter's face the day Susan had brought home a tiny black kitten and begged to be allowed to keep it. . .Whatever trouble the young man was in, he was appealing for help.

I wonder what sort of family squabble I'm walking into now? Camryn wondered. 'Of course,' she said. 'Won't you come in, Mrs Marlow?'

The woman sniffed, but condescended to come inside. The expression of pathetic gratitude in the young man's eyes was almost payment enough, Camryn thought.

'I'd like to go to my room,' Mrs Marlow said stiffly. 'It's bad enough to be shuffled off to a boarding-house instead of staying with my own flesh and blood——'

Boarding-house? Camryn thought.

'Mother, I've explained that we just don't have room in our apartment.' The young man turned to Camryn. 'I'm sharing an apartment with three other guys while I finish my residency, and I can hardly ask my room-mates to move out for the weekend. And we don't have an extra——'

'John, I do not care to hear you discuss our family problems with strangers. Mrs Hastings, I would like to retire to my room.'

Camryn closed her eyes for an instant, and pictured the master bedroom, with the bed stripped but not yet made up with fresh sheets. But the front bedroom was worse; in her fit of cleaning fever this morning she had even taken the curtains down to be washed. She fleetingly considered the other two guest-rooms and dismissed them. They were certainly not grand enough to please Mrs Marlow. No, it would have to be the master bedroom.

'Of course,' she said soothingly. 'But perhaps you'll sit down and have a cup of coffee while I put the finishing touches to your room?' She gestured towards the living-room and held her breath.

Mrs Marlow sniffed again, but she allowed herself to be nudged towards the living-room. She stopped in the doorway as Patrick McKenna rose from his chair. 'Are you Mr Hastings?'

Camryn wanted to swear. For an instant, she'd forgotten all about Patrick McKenna, but of course he would be there to see this. Of all the things he might have witnessed at the Stone House, Mrs Marlow was the worst of her nightmares.

'Sorry,' he said easily, 'but I'm afraid that honour isn't mine.' He came across the room to Camryn. 'Mrs Hastings——'

She said, under her breath, 'Look, I have to take care of my guest first. If you'll just be patient till I get her coffee and make up her bed——'

'Do you always leave these things till the last minute like this?'

'I don't run a sloppy business! I didn't even expect her till tomorrow.'

His eyebrows went up.

Camryn sighed. 'I suppose that sounds even worse, doesn't it? But I promise I can explain. Give me ten minutes and I'm all yours. . .' Then she felt herself start to flush again.

He pulled a heavy gold watch out of his waistcoat pocket. 'I'm charmed, but——'

'Not that I'm trying to keep you around for personal reasons!' she snapped.

'Of course you aren't. And I'd love to stay, just to hear what you say next, but I have an engagement tonight. I'll have to see your books another time.' He was gone before she could even offer to bring her records to the bank on Monday.

An engagement? He must have a date with the blonde, Camryn thought. No man would dare keep her waiting. Or was his date just an excuse? Had he changed his mind altogether about helping her?

I must look like a careless fool, she thought—the kind who takes reservations and then forgets them. Some businesswoman I must look like. Damn all the Mrs Marlows of the world!

The back door banged and Sherry came in, singing an old ballad, off-key but with enthusiasm. She stopped when she saw Camryn in the hallway. 'Guess what,' she cried. 'Proust worked after all—I found a new man in the college library.'

Mrs Marlow appeared in the wide-arched doorway between hallway and living-room. 'Young woman,' she said sternly to Camryn, 'I really must insist that this animal be removed instantly. I cannot abide cats.' She turned on her heel and majestically retreated to a chair beside the fireplace, where she sat bolt upright, tapping her fingers on the upholstery.

'New guest?' Sherry asked unnecessarily. 'Charming sort, isn't she? I'll lock Ipswich up in my room for the duration. You don't mind if he comes over after dinner? My new friend, I mean, not Ipswich. Unfortunately, he didn't seem to have a buddy for you.' She grinned unrepentantly. 'But then, from what I saw pulling out of the driveway as I was coming in, you did pretty well yourself today. Tell me, what were you reading in the park to attract *his* attention, Camryn—Casanova's memoirs?'

CHAPTER THREE

CAMRYN didn't sleep well, of course, and when the alarm clock gave its characteristic asthmatic wheeze, as it always did just before shrieking at her, she was already sitting on the edge of her bed with her hand on the button. She yawned and went to push aside the curtains. The pair of dormer windows in her bedroom looked out over the front of the house, towards the rising sun. Today, unfortunately, there was no sun to see—just the dim grey softness of a summer rainstorm, blurring the outlines of the world. On most days from her top-floor windows she could peek between the houses down the street and see Lake Michigan sparkling in the distance. Today the water was just another shade of drab grey, a reflection of the dark clouds.

Camryn sighed and pulled her cotton nightshirt over her head. No comfortable shorts and sandals today, or battered, soft jeans, either. She wasn't going to face another one of those contemptuous looks from Mrs Marlow if she could help it.

The sound of the shower woke Susan, who wandered in while Camryn was getting dressed and sat cross-legged at the end of the big bed, clutching her ragged teddy bear. 'Ipswich is lonely shut up in Sherry's room,' she announced. 'I can hear him. Can I go play with him?'

'Not till Sherry wakes up. And it's Saturday, so it might be a while.' Sherry's young man from the university library had come by last night as promised, and they had gone to one of the campus coffee-houses. Camryn didn't even know what time Sherry had come home; she herself had not gone to sleep till after midnight, but it wasn't unusual for Sherry to arrive with the morning newspaper.

'Stupid Mrs Marlow,' Susan grumbled. 'Ipswich doesn't like to be shut up.'

'That's quite enough, Susan. You have a right to like cats; other people have a right not to. And, whether we agree with them or not, we have to treat our guests with respect.'

Susan grumbled. Privately, Camryn agreed with her; Mrs Marlow alone was as aggravating as three ordinary guests, and so far she hadn't earned much respect. Thank heaven, Camryn thought, that she would be spending most of her time this weekend with her son, away from the Stone House. He'd be picking her up in a couple of hours, right after she had her breakfast—in bed, as she'd requested. And if it wasn't delivered to her door on the dot of the hour, there would be trouble. It didn't take a crystal ball to foresee that.

Camryn tied her hair back with a silk scarf that matched her slim, high-waisted trousers and said, 'Come on, Susan. You can help me make Danish.'

Outside, the clouds rumbled and the rain fell softly, but the two of them worked companionably in the brightly lit kitchen, Camryn shaping the soft, cheese-filled dough into circles, and Susan topping each pastry with strawberry jam. Her spoonfuls were sometimes uncertain, and their placement approximate at best, but she was having a great deal of fun. Besides, thought Camryn, we can pick out the best-looking two for Mrs Marlow, and eat the irregular ones ourselves.

When the doorbell chimed just as the first pan of Danish went into the oven, Camryn felt something very near panic. It can't be that late, she thought. Unless the rainstorm knocked out the power last night, and made my clocks all wrong. . .

But it wasn't John Marlow who had rung the bell. For an instant as she opened the door she thought she was imagining things. Surely it wasn't really Patrick McKenna, standing in a puddle on her front porch, with his hair so wet that it was plastered flat against his head? He was wiping raindrops off his face. . .

'You're soaked.' That was a stupid thing to say, she told herself. The important thing is, he's here. He didn't give up on me after all. But on Saturday? At this hour?

'There was a damned cloudburst the instant I got out of the car,' he growled.

'Glad you enjoyed it,' Camryn murmured. 'I arranged it on purpose just for your entertainment.'

He stared at her for an instant and then started to laugh. It was a very pleasant sound, she thought. He ought to do it more often.

'Come in,' she said. 'Make yourself at home. Drip wherever you like. I'm a bit busy with breakfast at the moment, so if you'd like a cup of coffee in the living-room while you wait——'

'Can I watch instead?' He sounded almost like Susan for an instant.

It caught her off guard, and she smiled at him almost as she would have at the child. 'Sure you can.'

It wasn't until they got to the kitchen that it occurred to her why he was so interested. Of course, she thought. He wants to see how things operate, and if I really am as disorganised as I looked yesterday.

Susan was standing on a chair beside the centre island, absorbed in decorating the second panful of Danish. She was working earnestly, her tongue stuck out in concentration, and she didn't even look up as they came in. Camryn took one look at the pan and said, 'Susan, a spoonful, for heaven's sake! You don't cover the whole top of the Danish——'

'But I like a lot of jam,' Susan said reasonably. Her eyes fell on the man following her mother.

'So do I,' he confided. 'We didn't really get a chance to meet yesterday, did we, Susan?'

'You're all wet,' she said.

'One thing about the Hastings women,' he muttered. 'They're observant.'

Camryn handed him a towel. 'This is Mr McKenna, Susan.'

Susan tried the name out, and stumbled over her tongue. Patrick McKenna leaned over the island and held out his hand. 'How about calling me Patrick?' he said. 'It'll be easier.'

Susan grinned at him and licked a spot of strawberry jam off her palm before putting her sticky little hand into his. He didn't flinch.

That's just great, Camryn thought; obviously her shyness yesterday was a fluke because she was so tired. Now my daughter is on a first-name basis with the man who's going to throw us out of our house. . .That's not fair, she reminded herself. After all, he did say he'd help.

She watched as he looked around, obviously assessing her kitchen. Copper pans gleamed under the bright lights above the island; blue and white tiles lined the counter-tops. Against the windows, beyond the lacy white curtains, raindrops splashed from the dingy sky, but inside, it was warm and bright. He sighed. 'It's unbelievably attractive in here, you know. I didn't expect a kitchen like this in an old house.'

'We started renovating it as soon as we moved in. You should have seen it before.'

'Who designed it?'

'I did. We couldn't afford an architect, so. . .' She rescued the pan of Danish from Susan's culinary talents and gave her a scrap of leftover dough to play with. 'I can hardly believe you're here.'

He grinned. 'Because you're so delighted to see me again, right?' He finished mopping water out of his hair and handed her the towel. 'You missed me—perhaps even dreamed of me?'

'You can say that again,' Camryn said drily. 'Mostly nightmares where large groups of men—all with your face—sternly ordered me from my house into a frozen wasteland deep in snow. Is that why you're here today?'

'Sorry to disappoint you, but it's nothing so crude. You did say I could look over your books.'

'On Saturday? Whatever happened to banker's hours? Nine to three, and Wednesday afternoons off to play golf?'

'That's a libellous rumour. Only the chairman of the board gets by with that.'

'Perhaps, but you don't strike me as average——'

'Thank you. I try very hard not to be ordinary, you see, because I plan to end up as the chairman of the board.'

'Still, isn't working Saturdays a little above and beyond the call of duty?'

His eyebrows raised. 'If you don't want me, Mrs Hastings, just say so. I do have other clients, you know.'

Including the glitzy blonde who'd been outside his office yesterday? Perhaps, she thought, he was working today to make up for the extra hours he'd spent at lunch yesterday. . .

'Sorry,' she said. 'Of course I want you.' She caught herself just as he started to smile, and added briskly, 'My financial records are in the top drawer of the desk.' She turned away to take the first pan of Danish out of the oven.

'Patrick,' Susan demanded, 'come see the funny cat I made.'

'Susan, Mr McKenna didn't come to play with you. . .'

But he was already beside the little girl's chair, approving the dough sculpture, and then forming another scrap into a caricature of a dog, which made Susan giggle. 'Don't you think we could descend to first names, too. . .Camryn?' he said over his shoulder.

'I'll admit that when you're playing with Susan you both seem about four years old.'

'Yes, we have so much in common,' he murmured. 'For one thing, our absorbing interest in dough. . . Where did you say you keep your records?'

He settled himself at the table in the breakfast nook and soon had every financial record she possessed spread out for inspection. Her entire business life lay open to his scrutiny.

Camryn tried not to dwell on what he was finding, or what he might think of it all. Instead, she drizzled icing over the hot Danish and got Mrs Marlow's breakfast-tray ready. As she was carrying it up the stairs she was astounded to meet Sherry coming down. On a normal Saturday, even without a late date the night before, Sherry might sleep till noon and then lounge around the house in her bathrobe till mid-afternoon, unless she was helping Camryn clean. Today she was already dressed, in a very nice skirt and brightly printed blouse instead of her usual jeans, and with her hair done——

Camryn stopped in the middle of the landing. 'Is that eye make-up I see?' she said, doing her best to sound impressed. 'On Saturday morning? And after a hot date last night, too?'

Sherry only smiled. 'I thought perhaps I'd add a little touch of elegance to a dull day.'

'Why? Are you going out?'

'No. I just didn't want to cause you any more trouble by letting Mrs Marlow see my ratty housecoat. Want me to take her breakfast in?'

Camryn handed over the tray without a moment's hesitation. 'I don't know why you're auditioning for sainthood today, but I'm not going to argue with my good fortune. It must have been quite a date last night if he left you in this frame of mind.'

Sherry only smiled, squared her shoulders, and marched up the stairs to Mrs Marlow's door. Camryn retreated to the kitchen, shaking her head.

A couple of minutes later, Sherry came in. 'I'm here to collect my reward,' she announced. 'After that skir-mish, I deserve one. Hand over the Danish, lady——' She saw Patrick at the breakfast-table and stopped dead. One eyebrow lifted enquiringly.

Susan flung herself down from her chair. 'Sherry's up!' she announced. 'I'm going to play with Ipswich, Mommy.'

Camryn said, 'Wash your hands first——' But the child was gone.

'Don't fuss,' Sherry said as she reached for the coffee-pot. 'Ipswich won't mind a little strawberry jam and cream cheese on Susan's fingers. In fact, he'll probably give her a full bath.' She was still watching Patrick.

Camryn introduced him. Sherry looked at the mass of papers on the table and said, 'Tax auditor?'

He grinned. 'Banker.'

'Oh, that's certainly good news, because Camryn and I make it a rule never to date tax men, no matter how gorgeous they are.'

Camryn's jaw dropped. 'That is not——' she began.

Sherry smiled vaguely. 'Isn't Lady Marlow's son due any time? I'll take my Danish into the living-room, darling, and guard the front door. It would be such a shame if you were interrupted.' She added, under her breath, 'And you talk about my hot dates, Camryn, dear.' She drifted off.

Camryn put her hands on her hips. 'I cannot believe that she actually said that!' she began furiously. 'As if we were—as if I would. . .' She sputtered to a stop and then added firmly, 'Sherry's not normally quite that dizzy.'

'She didn't look so dizzy to me,' Patrick mused. He had risen to shake hands with Sherry, and now he was sitting sideways at the breakfast-table, his chair pushed back, toying with a pencil as he looked up at her.

Camryn's breath caught in her throat. For the briefest of instants, she found herself wondering what it would be like to feel the caress of those long fingers against the sensitive skin of her throat. They would be strong, and yet gentle, she was sure of that. . .

'She got out of here with a plate heaped with Danish, and I'd say that indicates she knew what she was doing.' Patrick eyed the pan hopefully.

Camryn swallowed hard. I am relieved, she told herself. He might be a very good-looking man, but there is no sense in complicating things. Poor Sherry—all her matchmaking efforts were wasted, because he didn't even notice what she was suggesting!

She turned her back on him and started to clear up the mess Susan had left on the counter.

'I wouldn't consider it a bribe if you offered me one of those,' he added.

Camryn looked him over. 'You wouldn't? Then perhaps it isn't worth it to bother.'

'Just one, for a starving man,' he said as if he hadn't heard her. 'I'm not ill-mannered enough to beg for a plateful.'

She got him the Danish, and a cup of coffee, too. 'Just to save you the bother of asking for it,' she said acidly as she set the cup down beside him.

He only smiled and turned back to his paperwork, and she bit her tongue. It certainly won't hurt me to feed the man, she thought. It is his day off, after all, and he's trying to do me a favour.

She tried to be quiet as she moved around the kitchen, cleaning up the mess, but her eyes kept straying to him. He was awfully silent, she thought. What was he finding?

He rubbed the back of his head once, slowly, as if it ached, and she found herself studying the funny way his hair had dried after the unexpected shower, curling in tiny ringlets at the nape of his neck.

The kitchen was soon spotless, with every nook and crack scrubbed clean, and still he didn't look up. Camryn found herself wiping up non-existent spills, just to keep her hands busy. She had long since heard the front doorbell, and at least a quarter of an hour later the sounds of Mrs Marlow's departure with her son. Sherry had not come back to the kitchen.

She probably thinks we're in a clinch out here,

Camryn thought, and she's graciously keeping Susan out of the way!

She tried to fight back a yawn. Last night had been a bit frantic, as she'd tried to catch up on the cleaning in the couple of hours while Mrs Marlow was out to dinner with her son.

'This business involves long hours, doesn't it? And very hard work.'

Camryn turned around quickly. What had made Patrick say that? To all appearances, he hadn't taken his eyes off the ledger he was studying.

'Yes, but then most things worth doing are hard work.' You might as well be honest, she told herself. 'And I caused the long hours for myself yesterday—if I hadn't been lazy all day, I'd have been done long before Mrs Marlow arrived, which, by the way was a day earlier than her reservation.'

He didn't answer. Finally he sighed and pushed his chair back.

'Well?' Camryn asked.

'Oh, your records are meticulous. Of course, that's not the same as saying you're a mortgage lender's dream. I'm sure you've been considering your options since yesterday.'

It wasn't exactly a promising beginning, Camryn thought. She squared her shoulders. 'Yes, I have. And if you're going to suggest again that I move out——'

'I wasn't planning to.'

She blinked. 'Do you mean you've actually changed your mind?'

'About your financial status? No. About your ability to get a loan? Probably not. About you, and your general level of stubbornness—yes.'

She poured herself a cup of coffee and sat down

opposite him at the small table. 'Thanks for the compliment.'

'It wasn't meant to be one. But I give you credit for being realistic, too—sometimes—which is why I'm sure you've been thinking about it.'

'Do you have a recommendation?'

'Have you considered marrying a wealthy man who wants you to have a hobby?'

'That was uncalled for.'

'I know. Sorry.' He broke off a section of Danish and ate it thoughtfully. 'Have you ever thought of doing anything else? I know, you told me that you're not trained for anything. But there's no reason you couldn't start now. You're certainly smart enough to get any sort of education you want.'

She stared down into her cup. 'I've taken some courses at the college—accounting, business management. It was just things to help me get started with the bed and breakfast. I'd like to go on, but at the rate of one class a term, it looks pretty hopeless, and that's all I can manage. So I decided that when Susan's in school all day, and I won't have to hire a sitter all the time——'

'But that's still a while off?'

She nodded. 'Two years. And then it will probably take three more till I can get a degree. I have to live somehow in the meantime, Patrick——'

'You're taking a class now?'

She shook her head. 'Not during the summer—it's my busiest season.'

'What do you want to do after you finish your degree?'

'I want to run a bed and breakfast!' The cross-examination was beginning to irritate her. 'Patrick, I've been taking classes for two and a half years, and I'm still considered a fresher. How should I know what else I might like to do?' No sooner were the words out than she regretted them. 'Look, I'm sorry I snapped at you. It isn't your fault. But I really don't know—it seems so far away. Something in business, I think. At least it fits with what I'm already doing.'

He nodded. 'Fair enough. I didn't mean to nag. But what puzzles me is why you didn't do this before. I can't understand why you didn't go to college.'

'I didn't need a degree.' There was a trace of bitterness in her voice. 'I had a marriage licence.'

'But surely Mitch, with all his education, understood the value of——'

She walked across the kitchen to get the coffee-pot, not because she wanted more, but so she didn't have to look at him just then. 'The important thing at that moment was getting Mitch through his internship and residency and into practice. There would be plenty of time to think about me, later. And if I decided to stay at home and raise six kids instead, it was no problem. By then, he'd be well-established and we wouldn't need a second salary. . .'

Her voice cracked just a little. I am not going to cry, she told herself. I will not give him the satisfaction.

Patrick said gently, 'But there wasn't any time, was there?' He had followed her across the kitchen, so quietly that she didn't know he was there until he spoke.

She shook her head.

He put a hand very gently on the back of her neck. His fingers were warm against the tense muscles. 'You were awfully young when you were married, weren't you? You looked about eighteen.'

She nodded. Then she frowned. 'How would you know?'

'I saw your wedding picture in the living-room yesterday. Were you high-school sweethearts?'

'No. But close. Mitch was several years older than me—he and my brother were room-mates one year in college. We were married right after I finished high school.' She closed her eyes. The gentle friction of Patrick's hand on the back of her neck was soothing, comforting. She'd been right about the strength in his fingers, she thought idly. 'I've been thinking about what I could do,' she said slowly. 'And I just don't know.'

Patrick didn't comment. 'We talked about your family yesterday, but what about Mitch's relatives?'

'His father died when he was in medical school. His mother lives in Tucson. She's financially comfortable—at least enough to fly up here every year to visit us on Susan's birthday, but——'

'But you wouldn't want to owe her any favours.' It was gentle.

Camryn nodded, grateful for his perception. 'She's never even asked what sort of financial state Mitch left me in, and I get the feeling that she thinks the bed and breakfast is just something I do to make me feel important. And as for Mitch's sister—the last time I saw her, she hit me up for a loan, so I don't think she'd be much help.'

Patrick was smiling. 'No, I can see that.'

That smile, she thought, was enough to make the average woman light-headed. It certainly made the kitchen lights look dim. . .

'Nevertheless,' he said gently, 'it's going to have to come from somewhere. Is there anyone you might borrow from? Mitch's friends?'

'They all have successful practices now. But——'

'Have you kept in touch?'

'Not really,' she admitted. 'Christmas cards—that's about all.' She frowned. 'There is one I could ask, I suppose. He and his wife stayed here at the Stone House last year when he came back to the university to apply for a job. They seemed to enjoy themselves, and she was very interested in the house. They're living here in Lakemont now, and I suppose they might. . .' Her voice trailed off. It sounded like a very weak possibility, when she put it like that.

'It's worth a try, Camryn. It's not as if you'd be asking to borrow the whole amount, you see. I'll hold up the paperwork till you've talked to him.'

He picked up another Danish from the basket she'd left on the counter.

His problem is solved, Camryn thought irritably. He's not the one who has to call up that man and ask for cold cash!

'Help yourself,' she said coolly. 'And as long as we're talking about loans, you wouldn't happen to have a little cash tucked aside that you'd like to invest in a solid small business, would you, Patrick?'

'Not exactly. Why?'

'I'm doing my best to co-operate, you see—trying to find people who might loan me money. If I just had some cash, I could finish off the top floor of my garage into a guest-house. It would double my receipts, and——'

'Only if you had twice as many guests. How many do you have today?'

'Just Mrs Marlow,' she admitted reluctantly. 'But it's still a good idea. Guests come in hordes, you know. When the university has a special event, I have to turn people away. It would be a good opportunity for you——'

'Is that why you went to all this trouble?' He waved the Danish under her nose. 'To hit me up for a personal loan? My mother always warned me the surest way to a man's wallet is through his stomach. Did I get that right?'

'Not quite. And in case you've forgotten, I had no idea you were coming this morning, so all this work, as you put it, couldn't possibly have been done with you in mind.'

'Too bad.' It didn't sound as if it bothered him. 'In any case, don't look to me for a personal loan.'

'I'm disappointed. I thought bankers always had money.'

'So did I,' he said easily. 'That's why I chose the profession—it seemed only reasonable that hanging around where all the money is would help me acquire some, you see. So far it hasn't worked very well.'

'You seem to have plenty of cash to invest in a Mercedes,' Camryn pointed out.

Sherry peeked around the door. 'Is it safe to come in?' she asked in a stage whisper. She was carrying Mrs Marlow's discarded breakfast-tray, and beside her was Susan. The child's outfit looked as if she were going to a costume party as a rainbow, but at least she was dressed. Around her neck was the black cat, who was apparently pretending to be a fur stole. Susan marched across the room to show Ipswich off to her new-found friend.

Camryn seized the opportunity to glare at Sherry, who smiled and set the tray down. The basket of Danish had not been touched; a half-cup of coffee had been poured and left to grow cold.

Camryn sighed and started to clean up the mess. The work of producing Mrs Marlow's breakfast hadn't irritated her, but the waste did. 'Watch out,' she warned

Patrick over her shoulder. 'Just because Ipswich lets Susan drag him around like a rag doll doesn't mean he'll hold still for that sort of treatment from anyone else.'

But the warning was in vain; Ipswich was already snuggled into Patrick's arms, with his neck stretched out so an expert hand could more easily scratch his throat. Camryn could hear his rough, deep purr from half-way across the room.

'Ipswich likes you,' Susan announced. 'I like you, too, and so does Sherry. Does Mommy like you?'

'Of course she does,' Patrick murmured.

Camryn glared at him.

He winced, and added under his breath. 'Well, maybe not. Three out of four isn't bad.'

'Are you going to take my mommy out on a date? Sherry thinks you are.'

'No.' Camryn's voice was firm.

At the same instant, Patrick said, 'Actually, I wouldn't mind.'

He wouldn't mind, Camryn thought. Of all the things he could have said, that was the least enthusiastic response she could think of. He could have said that perhaps some time he would. He could even have said that he'd like to, but that business and pleasure didn't mix. But, of course, if he had said either of those things he would probably have been afraid that Camryn might think he actually meant it. Well, she'd leave him in no doubt of that!

'It's very kind of you,' she said frigidly, 'but I hope you'll ignore Susan completely. I think she has simply been listening to Sherry too much.'

Sherry didn't seem to hear. 'I'll even baby-sit,' she offered brightly. 'How about tonight, Patrick? There's a good movie on at the Galleria. Camryn's been wanting to see it, but it's kind of scary and she needs a strong shoulder to lean on.'

'Sherry!' There would have been a dire warning in Camryn's voice, if only it hadn't cracked in the middle.

Patrick McKenna bent over Susan to carefully hand the cat back, and as he stood up again Camryn realised that he was doing his best not to laugh. That made her even more irritable. He needn't think that she was so desperate for dates that she had to have her friend's and her daughter's co-operation!

'Seven o'clock, Patrick,' Sherry said airily. 'The movie starts at half-past, and you can go out for pizza or something later.'

Camryn's voice was a sheet of ice. 'I don't believe that Mr McKenna asked when he should come, Sherry——' Then she realised that she was only making a fool of herself with her protest; Patrick seemed to be enjoying the situation as the farce it was. Only Camryn was getting bent out of shape, and surely by now she ought to know what Sherry was capable of? She bit her tongue and gave her friend a cold little smile that promised reprisals later.

Sherry said promptly, 'I told Susan I'd take her to the library, Camryn. Would you move your car out of the driveway, Patrick, so I can get mine out? What did you do with your convertible, anyway? Though I suppose it's really not the weather to drive it in.' She reached for an umbrella from the stand behind the back door, captured Susan's hand with the ease of long practice, and ushered Patrick out of the door, still talking so smoothly that Camryn didn't even have a chance to say anything more.

Camryn stood in the centre of the big, quiet kitchen for a long moment. Then she swore, long and furiously— something she rarely allowed herself to do any more, now that Susan was big enough to imitate whatever she heard.

And Susan could be relied on to imitate—generally the very thing that her mother didn't want her to repeat. 'Are you going to take my mommy out on a date?' indeed! Susan hadn't thought of that one by herself. If Sherry had spent all week thinking of a way to embarras her friend she couldn't have found a more effective way.

'I'm going to get even, Sherry Abbot,' Camryn promised the empty room, 'if it's the very last thing I ever do!'

But as she went upstairs to change the sheets in Mrs Marlow's room, it wasn't Sherry she was thinking of any more. It was the movie she wanted to see, and the moment, before the whole ridiculous situation had got out of hand, when she had found herself thinking about how much fun it would be to see it with Patrick McKenna.

CHAPTER FOUR

SHERRY was properly apologetic. 'I had no idea it was really important,' she said mildly, after Camryn had explained just why, if she ever pulled such a stunt again, Sherry could expect to be not only evicted from her apartment, but thrown bodily from the top-floor windows of the house.

'You didn't know it was important?' Camryn asked unbelievingly. She stopped cutting up Susan's hamburger and waved the knife threateningly in Sherry's direction. 'He was sitting here inspecting every bill I've had in the last three years, every cancelled cheque I've written, and every rental receipt I've issued, and you thought it was just an excuse to share my company? Sherry, you total nitwit!'

'Well, some men have a lot of trouble working themselves up to asking for a date,' Sherry said reasonably. 'I thought he was one of them, from the looks of things. He certainly wasn't making much progress, and you weren't helping matters a bit.'

Of course, she thought, Sherry hadn't been in the bank yesterday. She hadn't seen the glitzy blonde clinging to Patrick McKenna's arm, or she would have realised that he had no trouble along those lines. 'The failure to make progress,' she said icily, 'stemmed purely from a lack of interest.'

'That's why I gave him a push——'

'A *mutual* lack of interest, Sherry. For all I know, the man's married.'

Sherry got up to pour herself a glass of milk and to investigate the contents of the refrigerator. 'I don't think so; he didn't have that married look about him. Are you going to eat here, Camryn, or wait and have pizza or something with Patrick after the movie? Or maybe he'll take you some place really elegant——'

Camryn closed her eyes in pain. 'You can't seriously think I would go to a movie with a man who didn't even ask me himself, even if he should happen to show up at seven o'clock, which I assure you he isn't going to do!'

'He'll come,' Sherry said comfortably. 'I'm willing to put a bet on it, if you like. What shall we do tonight, Susan, while your mom's out on her date?'

The truly annoying thing was that Sherry turned out to be right. Patrick McKenna was on the doorstep five minutes early, and when Camryn answered the bell he came to attention and snapped a salute. 'Reporting as ordered, ma'am,' he said.

Camryn tried to swallow a groan. I should have known better than to answer the door, she thought. But of course Sherry would have let him in, while I can get rid of him right here. 'You can't mean you took that nonsense seriously?'

'Don't you want to see the movie, after all? Sherry was telling me about it, and it sounded like a hit.'

He leaned into the narrow gap between the door and the frame, sliding a hand around the jamb. She'd have had to be heartless to close the door on his fingers, but she thought about doing it anyway.

'You don't have to take pity on me,' she said. 'I'm not going to pine away if I'm left at home for the evening, whatever Sherry thinks.'

'The shoe's on the other foot.'

'What does that mean?'

'It's Saturday night. I've got no date. You wouldn't want people to start talking about me, would you?' For a moment he sounded truly pitiful. 'Would you really prefer to stay home rather than come with me?'

'Depends,' Camryn mused. 'Why are you doing this?'

'Because I always like to know my clients on a personal level. Then I can serve them better.' There was a twinkle in his eyes that belied the pompous tone.

'Do you mean I might have a better chance at getting my loan if I came?'

'Are you offering a bribe, Mrs Hastings?' His smile flashed. 'Keep talking; this is getting interesting.'

Camryn did her best to pretend he hadn't said anything. 'If I could convince you of what a reliable, responsible person I am,' she said almost to herself, 'you might be inclined to give me the money. On the other hand, if you're bored, it would probably mean I'd never get the loan. I think, on the whole, I'd be better off to stay home tonight and tend to my business. You certainly can't hold that against me.'

'You really shouldn't be rude to me——' he began.

'I know,' she said, in her best shrinking-violet voice. 'You have my fate in your hands, you rogue——'

Sherry came into the hall from the kitchen, carrying a steaming mug. 'Didn't I hear the doorbell? Oh, hello, Patrick. You're right on time. I guess this means you're not married, after all, hmm?' She gave Camryn a cheeky grin and went up the first flight of stairs to the solarium.

'That girl is not going to live another week,' Camryn said between gritted teeth.

'Well, at least that would solve the problem of your mortgage. You wouldn't need one in prison.'

'It would be worth it. Look, I appreciate the kind thought about the movie, but it really isn't necessary.'

'Responsible, reliable people don't make dates and then break them.'

'This isn't a date, and I didn't make it. It's a manipulation, and neither of us would enjoy it——'

'I understand why you're wavering about coming with me. You have quite a choice of entertainment for the evening,' Patrick said blandly. 'You can go to the movie, where you won't even have to make conversation with me, or you can stay home and listen to Sherry.'

There was a long instant of silence. Camryn sighed. 'You do have a way of putting things into perspective, McKenna. All right—give me five minutes to change.' She pulled the door open. 'You can go up to the solarium and listen to her gloat. And if you want to drop a little arsenic in her herbal tea, feel free.'

It took her ten minutes to change, the first half of which she spent staring with distaste at her wardrobe. Nothing she owned seemed quite appropriate; Patrick, she couldn't help but notice, had been wearing dark trousers and an open-necked shirt under a soft blue sports jacket. At least it wasn't a pin-striped suit, she thought, but it wasn't exactly casual, either.

Finally she decided that it would be better not to make too big a thing out of what was certainly not an important evening, so she pulled on an old pair of jade-green trousers and a moss- and jade-striped silk sweater from Sherry's extensive collection. Her conscience twinged a bit at the idea of borrowing the sweater without asking, but she soothed it by reminding herself that Sherry owed her a favour or two. Besides, Camryn thought, I'm certainly not going to shout down the stairs to ask if I can borrow it, and make Patrick McKenna think I'm going to any trouble for his benefit!

When she reached the solarium, Sherry was curled up on the couch, wrapped in a pink blanket that made her look as delectable as a strawberry parfait. 'Nice sweater,' she said, with an elfin grin. 'Where did you happen to find it?'

Camryn made a face at her.

'It took you long enough to decide what to wear.' Sherry turned back to the television screen.

For a moment, she thought Sherry meant that Patrick had changed his mind and gone away after all. There would be some relief in that, she thought. Then she realised how much of the room was being taken up by Patrick, sprawled on his stomach on the rug with a colouring book open in front of him.

Susan, kneeling beside him, was thoughtfully selecting another crayon. She looked up when Camryn came in and said kindly, 'Mommy's here now, Patrick, and she doesn't like to wait. You'd better go.'

He laughed and mussed her flaxen hair with a gentle hand and rose to his feet in one fluid movement. 'My popularity around here astounds me,' he murmured to Camryn. 'They can't wait to get rid of me.'

'You can help finish the picture next time,' Susan said generously.

'I'm sure Mr McKenna would be delighted—if he comes again,' Camryn said. 'Do I get a goodnight hug, Susan?'

'And now you're trampling on my ego, too,' Patrick complained downstairs as he held her jacket. 'I've never felt so unwanted in my life. All I was trying to do was be a good guy and do what was expected of me. I wouldn't have put it past Sherry to turn up at the bank on Monday morning with a picket sign if I hadn't come to-night——'

'That's a thought,' Camryn said. 'I could handcuff myself to the time-lock on the vault and go on a hunger strike until I get my loan.'

'And sell the story rights to the tabloid newspapers,' he agreed easily. 'Why didn't I think of that myself?'

Camryn groaned. 'I ought to have known you'd find a way to make money on it

'It's a wonderful idea. I'd been wasting my time appraising your furniture. You've got some that isn't bad, you know.'

'Quite a bit of it came with the house.'

'Have you considered selling it?'

'No. I'd just have to replace it. I can't run a bed and breakfast without beds and——'

'But you don't need all of it, surely? And it would help the cash flow.'

She stopped beside a dark-coloured car parked at the end of the driveway. It was just a couple of years old, and it was nice enough, but it was nothing like the flamboyant silver Mercedes. Camryn remembered that Sherry had said he hadn't been driving the convertible that morning, either. 'You're a fine one to talk about cash flow,' she said. 'You have two cars? And you can't loan me a bit of money?'

'It's not just a bit of money that you need, Camryn.' He shut her door and walked around the car to slide behind the wheel. 'And I don't own two cars—the convertible belongs to a friend of mine.'

A glitzy blonde friend, I'll bet, Camryn thought. Yes, that made sense; the car was just her style.

'Convertibles are not practical for this climate, actually,' he said. 'I wouldn't want to own one.'

'But as long as she wants to loan it to you. . .' It was a soft, insinuating statement.

He smiled. 'That's different. I make it a point not to insult anyone who wants to do me a favour.'

'I'll keep that in mind,' she said drily.

At the theatre, she offered to pay her own way. 'This is not a date, you know,' she protested as he handed over the cash and got two tickets. 'In fact, maybe I should be paying your admission, too——'

'Don't forget I've seen your financial statement.'

'I didn't say I was rolling in money. I just thought if favours made such an impression on you. . .'

He only smiled and urged her into line at the confectionery stand. 'Butter on your popcorn? I'm sure if you really thought about it, Camryn, you could come up with a much better offer than just a movie ticket.'

'You know, you really should grow a moustache, Mr McKenna,' she said tartly. 'It would fit right in with your character.'

He gave a villainous chuckle, handed her a box of popcorn, and ushered her into the auditorium, where he watched the movie in such a gentlemanly way that she might as well have been alone. Sherry would be horrified, Camryn found herself thinking, and then told herself firmly not to be an idiot. Would she really have preferred the sort of wrestling match that Sherry seemed to think was the hallmark of a good time? After all, Camryn herself had announced that it was not a date, and now she was irritated because he wasn't treating it as one!

No, she wasn't irritated, she told herself. Not exactly.

But it did sting a bit that he didn't even try to hold her hand. It might have been a long time since Camryn had dated on any steady basis, but it wasn't because she hadn't had the opportunity. And for Patrick McKenna to sit there munching popcorn as if he was taking his sister to the movies—or Susan—was annoying in the extreme.

She shifted a little in her seat.

'Are you scared?' he whispered. 'I forgot—you can put your head on my shoulder if it would make you feel better.'

'Thanks, anyway,' she hissed, and sat up straight.

His muffled chuckle was no consolation.

After the show, he took her to an avant-garde ice-cream parlour near the university campus. The twisted-iron tables and chairs were antique classics, but the soda fountain itself was a modern wonder of glass and stainless steel. Behind it, against a gorgeous antique mirror, was a row of neon sculptures, featuring everything from a stethoscope in a painful shade of purple to a hot-pink silhouette of a saguaro cactus.

Camryn blinked. 'It's unusual,' she managed to say.

'It's well-lit,' Patrick said, soberly. 'And it'll banish all the spooks from the movie. I don't want to have nightmares.'

They found a tiny marble-topped table in a secluded corner, with two high stools that were more comfortable than they looked, and he ordered double-chocolate sodas for them both.

'Is that why you offered me the use of your shoulder?' Camryn asked tartly. 'Because *you* were scared?'

'Of course. I would have found it very consoling if you had relied on me for comfort. In fact, I'd been counting on it all day.'

'Enough, Patrick. Sherry isn't around, so you don't need to perform.'

He dug into the soda with his long-handled spoon, and for a moment his long, dark eyelashes lay heavily against his cheekbones. A blinking neon sculpture of an ice-cream sundae cast a greenish glow across his face at irregular intervals, but even the garish light couldn't conceal the fact that he was a very good-looking man. Camryn was well aware that most of the women in the ice-cream parlour had taken at least a second look at her companion.

And that has nothing to do with anything, she reminded herself. They're welcome to him—as soon as I get my loan.

'Have you always had such shocking taste in movies?' he asked lightly. 'After what Sherry said about you needing company, I expected you to be a quivering mass of nerves after the opening credits. Instead, you were a rock and I was the one who needed soothing.'

'Sherry sometimes edits the world to fit her own romantic notions.' Camryn was proud of her steady voice. 'She thinks every woman needs a man, while I make a habit of standing on my own two feet—depending only on myself.'

'What would Mitch think of that?' His voice was careless.

It stung, and she was less than pleased to realise that it was the first time all evening she had thought of Mitch. 'It would be different if Mitch had lived,' she said stiffly.

Patrick spooned up a lump of chocolate ice-cream and inspected it. 'What was he doing in that small plane, anyway?'

The question annoyed her. 'People do fly, you know,' she said tartly. 'It isn't as though he was a daredevil, or something.'

'I didn't think it was likely that he was a wing-walker in his spare time.' It was quiet, and very polite. 'I just wondered where he was going, Camryn.'

'And why I wasn't with him?'

'That question had also occurred to me.'

There was no good reason for refusing to answer him. Finally, reluctantly, she said, 'One of Mitch's buddies had just gotten his pilot's licence and a new plane. He was a whiz-kid, and he'd started a business in his garage and made it big—very big. Anyway, Jack was taking a couple of his employees to Canada for a week to hunt, and he invited Mitch to go along, to celebrate his long-delayed entry into the real world of making money, Jack called it.'

'You didn't mind?'

She shook her head. 'Mitch needed a vacation. He was exhausted when he finished his residency. Besides, Susan was only a few months old, and I wouldn't have wanted to leave her.'

His eyes were dark with intensity; she could almost feel the weight of his gaze. She looked down into her glass, where the textures of ice-cream and soda water had created a Paisley pattern. He hadn't asked what had happened to the plane. Perhaps, if she just stopped there, he wouldn't ask. But she went on anyway. There was something deep inside her that demanded she tell him about the crash.

'There was a storm——' She shivered, involuntarily. 'Much worse than had been predicted. The plane went down in rough country, in a national forest up in Minnesota. It took nearly a week just to find them.'

'Hell, Camryn——'

'They hadn't survived the crash. That was some comfort. At least they didn't have to wait, and suffer.'

'I'm sorry.'

She swallowed hard. 'It was a long time ago.'

'Perhaps.' He sounded dissatisfied. 'But—you just accepted it? Just like that?'

She looked up at him again then. She was beginning to know that tone of voice. 'What else was I supposed to do? If you're going to suggest that I should have sued Jack's estate because he was flying the plane——'

'I wasn't planning to say anything of the sort, actually.'

She was chastened for a moment.

'But I suppose you could have made a case that a more experienced pilot could have avoided the crash.'

'Probably,' she agreed in a brittle tone. 'And after a year or two in court I could have collected about ten dollars, which was all Jack's company was worth by then. Without him at the wheel, it went downhill fast.' She sipped her soda. 'Which brings us right back to the problem we started with, you know. I still need that mortgage loan.'

There was a brief pause. 'I know,' he said. 'And I've been thinking about you all day.'

For an instant, Camryn's breath seemed to catch in her throat.

'You, and Susan. Nevertheless, the rules haven't changed since yesterday, and there's not a lot I can do about it.' He sounded dejected. 'It takes the bank president to make exceptions, so I think you should meet with him as soon as possible.'

She thought it over for a moment. 'Does that mean you're going to recommend that he make an exception for me?'

For an instant she thought he wasn't going to answer. He was frowning, and his fingertip was tracing one of the marble veins in the table-top as if it were the most important task he would ever perform. Then the dark blue gaze lifted to meet hers, and he said firmly, 'Yes, I am.'

A pleasant glow rose from the pit of her stomach. Relief, she thought, and happiness. She reached impulsively across the table and touched his hand. His fingers were cold from the frosty glass and the marble. 'Patrick, thank you! I knew there had to be a way——'

'Don't get your hopes up,' he said sternly. 'I'm not guaranteeing anything, Camryn, I'm just sending you one step up the ladder. And we still have to improve this application. You may have a sterling character, but Warren Stanford is more impressed by numbers that come out in neat little rows.'

She drew back. 'I don't quite see——'

'What you'll gain? Well, you certainly can't lose. I can't approve your application; he can. Whether he *will* is another question. He isn't known for bending the rules lightly. Can you get hold of your doctor friend this week? Once you have an answer from him, we can work out how best to present it to Warren.'

She nodded. 'I tried this afternoon. He was gone for the weekend, but he'll be calling me back.'

'All right. I'll hold up the paperwork till I hear from you. In the meantime, I suppose it wouldn't hurt to think of alternatives——'

'Like selling my furniture? Come on, Patrick——'

'All right, you made your point. But how about the china you used for coffee yesterday? That's good stuff, and worth quite a bit, and surely you could do without it?'

'It was my grandmother's,' Camryn said stiffly.

'Nevertheless, if it comes to that——'

She set her glass down on the marble-topped table with a crash. 'You're heartless, Patrick McKenna!'

'I'm trying to be businesslike.'

'Well, as long as we're talking about selling things, I'm sure Susan would have a little value on the black market, too—shall I sell her?'

'Camryn, you're going to have to be reasonable. The fact is, I can't simply wave a magic wand and make your financial problems go away——'

'I'm being reasonable! I work hard, and I'm quite willing to continue. I'm not asking for a miracle, just a fair chance!'

'You're going to have to take this seriously, and be willing to make some sacrifices.'

'Take it seriously?' She stared at him. 'Hell, you've got a nerve. Do you think I see this as some sort of joke? One you created because you were dying to meet me, I suppose! You and Sherry!' Words failed her.

'Camryn——'

'You're the one who's made all the hilarious suggestions! I've just been trying to stay calm, and show you that I can handle stress, that I can get through this and make it all work, if you'll only give me the opportunity to try. . .'

Her voice cracked, and to her own horror a tear rolled down her cheek and splashed into the remains of her soda.

That does it, she told herself. That's just exactly what you need to do—dissolve in tears and let him think that you're one of the clinging-vine types who can't manage to do anything more for herself than to carry a handkerchief——She didn't even have a handkerchief. She scrabbled through her handbag twice, cursing herself for having been in such a hurry to get dressed, before she gave up and sniffed defiantly a couple of times.

Patrick sighed and handed her a large white square that looked as if it had never been used.

Of course, she thought. The perfectly groomed banker never needs to blow his nose!

She would have thrown it back at him, except that her only alternative was to drape herself in her napkin and slink out. People were starting to notice, she saw out of the corner of her eye. There was a couple near the front door, eating banana splits, who had looked at her for a moment as if they couldn't quite believe what they were seeing.

She blew her nose, wiped her eyes, mopped her cheeks dry, and said, 'I don't suppose you want this back.'

Patrick looked at the damp handkerchief with faint distaste. 'Not exactly, no. Are you ready to leave?'

He's ashamed of me, she thought. So much for making a good impression on him. . . Not that it matters, really. And he's the one who's to blame. Telling me to be realistic—acting as if I thought the whole thing was a practical joke!

'I don't think we have anything else to say to each other, that's true.' She slid down from the high stool without waiting for his help and started for the door. He caught her hand and tucked it firmly into his elbow, as if to say that she was not going to make the scene any worse. Deep inside her, Camryn felt the stirring of a childish impulse for revenge. Just what would he do, she wondered, if she pulled away and told him in loud tones never to touch her again——

He stopped, suddenly, and said under his breath, 'Damn!'

She looked up at him, startled. It was an awkward position to be in, threading her way between the close-packed tables, her arm extended full-length behind her, and her hand held prisoner by a man who seemed, at the moment, to be imitating a lamp-post.

'My parents are sitting by the door,' he murmured.

Camryn followed his gaze and wanted to swear; he was looking at the couple who had appeared so startled when she had burst into tears.

'Well, there's no way out but through.' He pulled her closer and cupped his other palm over her hand, resting quietly in the crook of his elbow.

'Didn't the people in the Light Brigade say something like that?'

Patrick smiled ruefully. 'If they didn't, they should have.' He paused beside the small table nearest the door. 'Having a mad night out on the town, you two?'

The man at the table put down his spoon and said to the woman across from him, 'Now will you believe me, Kath? It's not a persecution complex; the kids *are* checking up on us. We can't even go out for a concert and a snack without running into at least one of them.' He stood up and flashed a smile at Camryn, his hand extended. 'I'm Dennis McKenna. My wife, Kathleen.'

Camryn would have recognised the smile anywhere. It was Patrick's, too, though she got the feeling that his father used it more often. She swallowed hard and gave him her hand, but she didn't meet his eyes as she murmured her name.

'Won't you join us?' Kathleen McKenna waved a hand at the table.

'And sit where, Mother?' Patrick asked bluntly. 'Besides, we're just going. Camryn's not feeling well.'

Camryn could have kicked him.

'Yes, I noticed earlier,' Kathleen said. 'It's been a terrible season for allergies, hasn't it?' She smiled a bit vaguely at Camryn. 'It's all the pollen sweeping up from the south-west, I suppose. Patrick, I was going to call you about the Fourth of July party next weekend. Are you bringing——' She stopped suddenly, as if, for the first time, she had really seen Camryn. '—someone?'

Darn it, Camryn thought. For a minute there, it seemed that I might actually hear her name! Then she told herself not to be an idiot; for all she knew, there might be a dozen glitzy blondes—or their equivalent—in Patrick McKenna's life.

'Bring all your friends,' Dennis said. 'She's talking about making it into a painting party.'

'It's logical,' Kathleen murmured. 'We could get the whole house painted in a weekend, that way.'

'It might appear to be logical,' Dennis told her, 'but it doesn't make a lot of common sense.'

Patrick smiled at them both and said he would let his mother know when he'd decided if he was bringing anyone to the party, and swept Camryn out. Her head was swimming.

'Did your mother really think I was having an allergy attack?' she demanded.

'Why? Are you worried about it?'

That puts me in my place, Camryn thought. Of course it doesn't matter what his mother thinks of me, and he's making very sure I know it. 'Absolutely not,' she said coldly. 'I'd much rather she think I'm an ill-mannered slob who likes to throw tantrums in public places!'

He smiled. 'Don't worry about that. If anything, she'll dress me down for treating you badly and making you cry. Maybe I should invite you to the Fourth of July party——'

'Don't put yourself out on my behalf.'

'It's purely self-interest, Camryn. If you'd agree to go

to the party with me, it would convince my mother that I'm not such a bad guy after all.'

'She didn't seem to be the sort you'd be frightened of.'

'Do you always make these snap judgements about people's characters?' he asked plaintively. 'You seem to think I'm wicked to the core, but I assure you——'

'Oh, you're a charming guy,' Camryn said. 'And I fully expect that your next helpful suggestion for raising money will be to take in some boarders with—how shall I say it? Flexible morals and lots of gentlemen friends, that's it.'

'Camryn, selling your china is not in the same league as running a house of ill fame.'

He was right, and she was momentarily ashamed of herself. She was silent for a couple of blocks, staring out of the window at the quiet neighbourhood. 'Sorry,' she said stiffly. 'But I don't think you understand, Patrick.'

'Yes, I do, better than you think.' The car turned into the driveway beside the Stone House, and he turned the engine off and came around the car to help her out.

'Thanks for the movie, Patrick.'

'I'll walk you to the door.'

Camryn swallowed the protest she had been about to make. Foolish, she told herself. What did she expect— that he would try to force his way into the house?

The light was on in the front hall, and it played games with the bevelled glass in the front door, slicing itself into twisted geometric patterns that looked other-worldly against the porch floor. Patrick took her key and unlocked the front door, but when she started to push it open his hand closed gently on her arm and turned her to face him.

'What——?' she was just starting to say when he kissed her.

His mouth was firm against hers, but not rough, not demanding. His palm slid gently down over her hair and came to rest at the nape of her neck, warm against her cool skin. His other hand was braced against the door frame above her head, almost as if he was trying to keep himself from touching her in any other way.

But the lack of bodily contact didn't translate to a lack of feeling, Camryn found. It merely concentrated all sensation to the two vulnerable areas he was touching, and from there tiny shock waves radiated out, overlapping and colliding with one another until not a single cell of her body remained untouched.

His tongue slipped gently between her lips, softly tracing the even line of her teeth. When, finally, he released her mouth, she found herself leaning against the door-jamb, her face turned up to his as if to prolong that last moment.

'You taste like chocolate ice-cream,' he said. His voice was no more than a teasing whisper.

'Are you sure that's me?' She didn't even hear what she was saying. 'You ate the same thing I did.'

His eyes lit softly. 'Perhaps I should try again, to be certain.'

She caught herself up short just as he reached for her, and fended him off, trying to sound amused. 'All right, would you like to tell me what that was all about, Patrick?'

He smiled down at her, eyes dancing. 'Don't you think Sherry will expect something of the sort?'

Her stomach contracted painfully for a second. Was that all? she thought, and then told herself not to be stupid. 'It really wasn't that sort of evening, you know.'

'She'd be awfully disappointed if you told her that. And you wouldn't want to fabricate something to satisfy her——'

'I wasn't planning to fabricate anything.'

'I'll take that as a compliment.'

'It wasn't one. Anyway, what does it matter what Sherry thinks?'

'I'd like her to get the idea that I'm capable of proceeding on my own.'

She nodded a little hazily and pushed the door open wide. She didn't quite understand, but she wasn't going to worry about it.

He didn't move. 'Camryn?'

She turned. He was holding out a small object that glinted in the light. 'Don't you want your key?' he asked gently. 'Or would you like me to keep it?'

CHAPTER FIVE

SHERRY was still in the solarium, tucked up in her pink blanket and watching television. She turned the set off just as Camryn came in. It must have been an old romantic comedy she was watching, Camryn concluded; she had seen that particular soft, warm glow on Sherry's face before.

'I wasn't waiting up for you,' Sherry said quickly. 'I was just ready to take my dishes down and check the locks before going to bed, when I heard the car in the drive and—well, I didn't want to interrupt you and Patrick.' She smiled sweetly. 'It was such a nice goodnight. . .'

Camryn bit her tongue, hard. Damn him! she thought; he'd been right again. She sent a curious glance towards the front door. It was funny that she'd never noticed before how much of the house could be seen from the solarium. The glass wall that closed the room off from the landing did nothing to interrupt the view. She could see the entire hallway, and as for the porch—Camryn could feel colour rising in her cheeks as she reconstructed what the scene in the doorway must have looked like from this angle.

'I'll have to remember that,' she muttered.

Sherry flashed her gamine grin. 'Next time, bring him into the living-room and close the door,' she suggested silkily.

Camryn ignored her. 'That view will come in handy in a few years, when Susan starts to date.'

75

'Perhaps I should do the child a favour on her thirteenth birthday and warn her about it.' Sherry pushed her blanket aside. 'She's sound asleep, by the way.'

'Good.'

'Lady Marlow is all tucked in, too. She doesn't want breakfast till late—her son wore her out today.'

'That's a blessing.'

'Yes, isn't it? I think he did it on purpose because he feels sorry for us, having to cope with her.'

'Actually, she hasn't been bad.'

'Speak for yourself, dear. You've just had too many other things on your mind.'

That was true enough, Camryn thought, even though the things that were on her mind weren't quite the ones Sherry thought.

Sherry turned in the doorway. 'Sweet dreams, Camryn. Oh, and don't fret about me seeing you kissing him. It was perfectly decent. He is quite the gentleman, isn't he?'

If there had been an ashtray handy, Camryn would have thrown it at her. Instead, she said gently, 'Yes, he is. He even introduced me to his parents tonight.'

And before Sherry could manage to close her mouth, Camryn slipped past her and went up the stairs to her room.

Stupid, she told herself. That was very stupid. There are better ways to put an end to Sherry's teasing, and all you managed to do was give her something else to speculate about.

She undressed in the dark, not even bothering to find a nightshirt, and slid gratefully between cool sheets. It had been an unbearably long day, and she was worn out.

'If someone had told you when you got up this

morning, Camryn Hastings,' she muttered, 'that you would finish off the day on your front porch in Patrick McKenna's arms, being quite thoroughly kissed, you'd have thought you were having a nightmare!'

And she hadn't exactly been in his arms, either, she reflected. He'd been very careful to keep it just a gentlemanly goodnight kiss, for Sherry's benefit. No more than that. . .

She fluffed her pillow into shape, but as soon as she put her head down on it her traitorous, overtired mind took her straight back to the front door, into his embrace. And this time it wasn't a very gentlemanly kiss. It was still soft and tender, but it was deeper, warmer, infinitely more seductive. And this time she was in his arms. In fact, he was carrying her up the stairs, and when they reached her room at the top he wasn't even out of breath, but she was gasping, more hungry for him than for oxygen——

'Oh, for heaven's sake!' she said crossly. She turned over and buried her face in the pillow.

It was as if arms had closed gently around her. The brush of the cotton sheet against her bare skin was like the stroking of a warm hand——

'What's the matter with you?' she accused herself.

—a warm hand gently caressing her, and strong arms that held her firmly, not with force, but with the knowledge that she wanted to be held securely against his body, while the world tilted crazily askew. . .

She reached up, breathing hard, and snapped the bedside light on. For a long moment she lay there staring at the quiet room, trying to impress on every level of her mind the undeniable fact that she was alone.

'You're acting like a sex maniac,' she muttered half-consciously, and winced at the very unexpectedness of what she had said.

For months after Mitch had died she had simply been numb about everything. Each day she did the things that had to be done, because her brain told her it was necessary; each night she lay alone in the bed they had shared, and slept because she was too exhausted not to sleep. But she had not felt anything; shock had kept her anaesthetised.

Then after a while she had started to feel things again—confusion about what had happened, and fear for the future, and sorrow for her loss, and tenderness and love for her child. She had started her business, and she had moved out of the big bedroom and up one floor, to a room she had never shared with Mitch. And though she lay awake sometimes and thought about him, after a while she had come to realise that her sexual longings had died with Mitch. She was glad. Life was hard enough as it was, missing him. It would have been just too complicated otherwise.

She had dated, of course, after a decent interval. Even her mother had told her she should. But she and Susan were a package, and it was inevitable that sometimes Susan had to come first. Camryn had found there weren't many men who really liked that idea. They tended to drift away, and she hadn't really missed them. It wasn't as if she felt a need for anything more than friendship.

But tonight—on the front porch, in Patrick McKenna's arms—there had been a stirring of that other self, the one she thought had died over three years ago when that plane crashed. . .

'Don't be such a dimwit,' she told herself sternly. 'Nothing happened. And you weren't even in his arms, really.'

You might as well have been, her conscience declared. It was a very thin line. And you'd better watch yourself in the future, too, Camryn Hastings. If you're going to start thinking about male company again, fine. There's nothing criminal about that, and Susan's older now—more independent. But there are a lot safer people around than your banker. Patrick McKenna is a land-mine in disguise. . .

She reached for her robe and went to check on Susan. The child's bedroom, just down the hall from Camryn's, was dim, with a pale pink night-light glimmering softly in one corner. Susan lay sprawled on her stomach, her blankets kicked aside, one leg stretched out over the side of the bed, her nightgown bunched and twisted by her restless movements.

The length of her startled Camryn. She's growing so fast, she thought sadly. My baby's gone, and soon my little girl will be a big one.

It had seemed a joke downstairs, when she had said that some day Susan would be kissing a boy goodnight on the front porch. But now it seemed uncomfortably near.

How will I handle it? she thought. How will I teach her what to do, and what to expect? Mitch would have told me what to do. A little girl misses her father, but a bigger girl needs him even more. . .

She stooped over the bed and straightened Susan out, tucking her under the blankets again. The child sighed and flung her arm out, and from under her pillow peeked a furry dark brown object. Camryn picked the stuffed toy up and held it for a long moment, while memories crowded in one after another. Mitch had brought Freddy Bear to the hospital the day after Susan was born. . .

Camryn put the bear down next to Susan, who shifted in her sleep and pulled it close to her chest and smiled a little.

It's all right, Camryn told herself. We have time.
Perhaps she's not in such a hurry to grow up, after
all. . .

The silver Mercedes convertible was parked in the space
nearest Lakemont National Bank's main door on
Monday morning. Camryn eyed it warily; if Patrick had
been driving it, she suspected, it would be tucked away
somewhere neatly in the far corner, out of the customers'
way. The fact that it was displayed so prominently
probably meant that the glitzy blonde was in the bank,
and if there was one person Camryn didn't really want
to run into today, it was that female.

But she didn't have much of a choice. She had to see
Patrick, and the sooner the better, no matter who else
might be outside his office.

She reached across to unfasten Susan's safety-belt.
'Leave your bag here,' she said as Susan reached for the
backpack that held her special shoes. 'We'll just stop at
the bank for a couple of minutes, and then I'll take you
on to class.'

Susan frowned, but she obediently slid out and held
Camryn's hand as they walked into the building. She
looked even taller today, Camryn thought with a sigh,
dressed for her gymnastics class in pink tights and
leotard. The outfit was almost new, but it wouldn't be
long before it was outgrown.

Camryn deposited John Marlow's payment for his
mother's weekend stay in her account, and turned
towards the executive offices. Susan trailed behind her,
unwrapping the lollipop the teller had given her.

Mr McKenna was in conference, the secretary said.
No, she wasn't able to predict when he might be
available, but if Mrs Hastings would care to wait. . .

Camryn sat down just outside his open office door, tapping her foot on the luxurious carpet and checking her wrist-watch at least every thirty seconds. She knew it was ridiculous to have assumed that he'd be standing at the door waiting, but somehow she had assumed that he would be expecting her.

He spent most of Saturday with you, one way or another, she lectured herself, and so you started feeling important!

Susan sucked thoughtfully on her lollipop and looked around. She'd never been past the tellers' windows before. 'Does Patrick live here?' she asked finally.

'No, dear. He works here—in that office.'

Susan stood in the doorway and inspected the room. 'He's not there.'

'He's probably in another office, behind one of those doors.'

'Can I go and find him? I'll knock.'

'No!' It was slightly shrill, and Camryn caught herself. 'He's busy—he'll come out to see us when he can.'

'But how does he know we're here?'

The logic of a four-year-old, Camryn thought, was sometimes enough to defeat the most sensible adult. She pulled a picture book out of her handbag, and Susan reluctantly climbed into the chair next to her and began to turn the pages. It was a well-loved story, and Susan knew it practically by heart.

Camryn's nerves tightened as time slipped away, and still the row of doors remained obstinately closed. Finally, she approached the secretary. 'I'll just have to leave a message for him,' she said. 'If you'll tell him I was here, and to please call me as soon as he can——'

Behind her, there was a little shriek, and a book went flying as Susan dashed across the lobby to a door that had opened silently. By the time Camryn turned, Susan was tugging at the sleeve of Patrick's dark grey suit. He bent and swung her up into his arms.

Sticky hands and all, Camryn thought miserably.

Then she saw the blonde woman beside him, every hair in place, her make-up perfect. Her fuchsia dress was carelessly elegant. She drew back a bit from Susan's enthusiasm, and turned to stare at Camryn.

'I guess I'm not as unpopular as I thought,' Patrick said. 'Come and meet Mr Stanford, Camryn.'

'Actually, I didn't intend——' She felt incredibly clumsy as she crossed the little lobby under the blonde's gaze. Here I am in my jeans, she thought, next to that vision. . .

'Who have you got there, Patrick?' It was a booming voice, and the man who appeared in the office door was built to match it. He was tall and thick-shouldered and massively constructed.

'One of our youngest depositors,' Patrick said. 'And her mother—I was telling you about Mrs Hastings earlier.'

Warren Stanford had a handshake that could cripple, and a way of wrinkling his bushy white eyebrows and looking straight under them and into the soul. It was terrifying, Camryn thought. She almost wanted to curtsy—or just to turn and run.

'Don't mind me.' The blonde's voice was a sultry purr. 'I'm just leaving anyway.'

Warren Stanford grinned. 'Now, Dianna,' he said pleasantly. 'You take care of the arrangements for the picnic, and let Patrick and me get back to work. And I'll see if I can't drag him home to dinner tonight so you can tell us all the details.'

The blonde's eyes went from Camryn to Susan to Patrick. 'You do that, Daddy.'

Daddy. Well, Camryn thought, that was no big surprise. 'I plan to end up as chairman of the board,' he had said. This went a long way towards explaining how he intended to pull it off.

Patrick shook his head. 'I'll try, Dianna, but I won't promise. We may have to make it some other night.'

'You're working too hard, my boy,' Warren Stanford said. 'Good thing there's a holiday coming up—that reminds me, Mrs Hastings. As a good bank customer, you should come to our picnic on Friday evening. It's just a little thank you for our favourite customers, right, Dianna?'

Dianna Stanford's eyes had sharpened to blue diamonds. 'Of course,' she said, and only another woman would have heard the ice under the polite words. 'Do come, Mrs Hastings. I think you'd find it an interesting change of pace.' She kissed the air beside her father's cheek and turned on her heel to leave the bank.

Warren Stanford chuckled. 'That young woman has a one-track mind,' he said. 'All she can think about is her picnic. Patrick told me you have a mortgage problem, Mrs Hastings. Come into my office and we'll talk about it.'

She met Patrick's gaze, and made no effort to conceal the panic in her eyes. 'I'm afraid I have another appointment just now. I only stopped because I need a minute with you, Patrick.'

His eyebrows raised. For a moment, she thought he was going to insist, and she looked at him pleadingly. Finally he said, 'This afternoon would be better, Warren. Camryn and I can finish up the paperwork over lunch so it's all ready for you to look at.'

The president glanced at his watch. 'I suppose that would work,' he said. 'I have a lunch appointment myself. I'll see you in a couple of hours, then.'

Camryn muttered as he went off to talk to the secretary 'Of course the chairman of the board can take two hours for lunch——'

'What's the matter with you, Camryn? I had him prepared—all in the mood to talk to you. Didn't your doctor friend come through?'

'In a manner of speaking, yes. Susan, come on, we'll be late to your class as it is. Patrick, when can I talk to you?'

Patrick turned towards the door, still carrying Susan. 'Right now. Over lunch.'

'Do you get two hours for lunch as well?'

'Is it going to take two hours?'

'Probably not. But my lunch on Mondays consists of sitting in the gym while Susan and eleven other little girls practise cartwheels, somersaults, and giggles.'

'You wouldn't consider missing one class to get your mortgage straightened out?'

She stopped beside her car. 'Believe me, Patrick, if I'd skipped the class and gone into his office you would be sorry.'

'All right, we can talk about it while we wait for Susan.' He slid into the passenger seat.

'Does this come under the heading of personal banking services?' Camryn didn't wait for an answer. 'One of our youngest depositors,' she muttered as she negotiated the few blocks to the gym. 'Have you been checking up on me, Patrick? If you've gotten it into your head to think it would help if I cashed in Susan's savings account. . .' She sighed. 'Well, it probably would. All ninety-three dollars of it.'

He whistled. 'Things are that bad, hmm? I thought you said the doctor was going to help you out.'

She didn't answer until she had parked the car. 'I'll take Susan in and be right back.'

He wasn't there when she returned to the car. She looked around irritably and saw him crossing the street from a fast-food restaurant, carrying a paper bag. 'I thought the discussion might go better over some food,' he said, and pointed to a park bench in a tiny patch of grass nearby. 'Would you care to join me in a cheeseburger and a Coke? It's the best I could do—the wine steward and the continental chef are taking the day off, I'm afraid.'

She pulled her feet up on the edge of the bench and hugged her knees while he unpacked the bag. It was a perfect summer day, with a gentle breeze balancing the heat of the sun pouring down on the concrete.

He handed her a sandwich. She took a bite out of it and said, 'You're very nice, you know.'

'I'm just softening you up. What happened, Camryn? The doctor obviously wasn't helpful, after all.'

She pushed a lock of hair out of her eyes, where the breeze had blown it. 'Oh, he was willing to be helpful. He stopped by this morning, and listened to my problem, and volunteered to guarantee my loan. And all I had to do was make sure I was available on the nights when he could get away from his wife.' She picked up her sandwich and looked at it without interest. 'He made it very plain what he expected.'

Patrick's jaw tightened. 'How charming of him.'

'He seemed to think I'd planned it,' she said drearily. 'As if I've been dreaming of him for the whole year since he stayed at the Stone House, and trying to find a way to get him back.'

'So you told him to get lost.'

'Of course I did.' She turned on him in fury. 'I suppose you think I should have agreed to it! Dammit, Patrick, it was disgusting, and nauseating, and——' she was almost in tears '—and I felt dirty, just listening to his sleazy suggestion that I sleep with him.'

He put his hand on her shoulder; she shrugged it off. 'Camryn, must you always assume that I'm the bad guy? Of course you were insulted. If you hadn't told him off, I was going to go wipe the floor with him myself.'

She bit her lip. She had jumped to conclusions, that was certainly true. But she couldn't quite bring herself to apologise, either. 'You couldn't do it,' said, finally. 'He's six feet four and he lifts weights——'

Patrick smothered a grin. 'All right,' he said. 'So I'd have tampered with the computer at his bank. Having his balance wiped out would probably hurt him more than a bloody nose would, anyway.'

She giggled. She couldn't help it.

His fingertips brushed against her hair, tentatively, as if he wouldn't be surprised if she slapped him. She sat very still instead, and eventually his hand came to rest on her shoulder and began to rub gently at the base of her neck, where the muscles were still tense.

Finally, reluctantly, she said, 'Susan's class will be over.'

'And she needs her lunch.' He pulled her to her feet. 'Is she a cheeseburger sort, too?'

Camryn shook her head. 'I'll take her home. It's easier.'

'But not nearly so much fun.' He came in with her, and Susan came flying across the gym to meet them. Patrick picked her up and swung her around until she collapsed in dizzy giggles.

'So what's next?' Camryn asked on the way back to the bank. 'Surely not talking to Mr Stanford this afternoon?'

Patrick shook his head. 'No, I think we should let it rest a while. I'll find an excuse to delay it.'

'The trouble is, I've got no idea what to do instead.'

He was quiet for a couple of blocks. 'The next thing is to let Warren get to know you personally,' he said finally.

'What good will that do?'

'Psychology. It's much harder to turn people down when they're a face and a family, not just a name on a piece of paper. Come to the picnic on Friday and be your most charming self——'

Camryn smiled ruefully. 'I'm amazed that you can say that with a straight face.'

Susan's head popped up over the seat. 'Picnic?' Her hands rested confidently on Patrick's shoulder.

Camryn shuddered. 'She's ruining your suit. And she had chocolate this morning, too——'

'No harm done.' He didn't even check for damage.

'You're good with kids, you know.'

'I had to be. It was a matter of survival. I'm the oldest of five.'

'Five? I heard your father say last night that he kept running into kids, but I thought——'

'That I was enough trouble all alone, right?'

'Something like that.'

Patrick grinned. She stopped the car in front of the bank, and he brushed a casual hand across her cheek. 'Don't fret, Camryn—I'm not out of ideas yet. See you Friday.'

'At the picnic.' She sighed. 'All right, if you insist.'

But, she realised as she drove home, he hadn't said

anything about taking her to the picnic—just that he would see her there.

What did you expect? she asked herself. The lovely Dianna will be there. And with her around, you'll be lucky if Patrick sees you at all.

She didn't stop to wonder if 'lucky' was quite what she meant.

She certainly didn't see anything of him all week. Not that she had much time to think about it; the Stone House was busy, with several days when all four guest-rooms were in use. Camryn had her hands full, and Sherry wasn't much help; she carried trays and changed beds when asked, but it was in a vague sort of way. Sherry's saintly behaviour of the weekend had obviously been too good to last, Camryn told herself on Friday morning as she readied the two back bedrooms for the guests who would arrive late that afternoon. Then she went down to the breakfast-room and plunged into the pile of paperwork that always seemed to be hanging over her head. She had half an hour before picking Susan up at nursery school, which was just enough time to take care of the bills. . .

The couple who had reserved the master suite for the weekend had requested afternoon tea upon their arrival; it was a service Camryn was happy to provide, because it was easy to do, and people would pay the earth for it without complaining. But today she would much rather take Susan to the park, and soak up some much-needed sunshine, and restore her energy level before going to that damned picnic tonight.

The invitation was pinned up to the cork-board above her desk. 'It's the first picnic I ever got a printed invitation to,' Camryn muttered, staring at it. It was a good quality printing job, too, on heavy paper. But of course the bank would do something of the kind; taking out an advertisement in the Lakemont *Chronicle* wouldn't be quite the thing. Besides, it was apparent that not every one of the bank's customers was invited. Camryn's invitation had obviously been an afterthought.

It had come in Wednesday's mail. 'I should be flattered that it was so prompt,' Camryn said under her breath. 'Two whole days' notice!' And as for the personal note written at the bottom by Dianna Stanford herself——

'Patrick has told me how disappointed he will be if you don't come,' it said.

Camryn took the invitation down from the cork-board and stared at it. '"Patrick has told me,"' she mused. 'I see he must have gone to dinner that night after all.'

And Dianna was making no effort to hide the fact that if it hadn't been for Patrick, Camryn Hastings would not have been invited. 'It would be my pleasure to refuse,' Camryn informed the invitation, and then put it back on the cork-board with a vicious stab of a thumb tack. 'If only I could.'

The telephone rang at her elbow. If it was a friend wanting to chat, Camryn decided, she would have to be ruthless. There was just too much work yet to be done.

Instead, it was the young woman who had reserved the master suite for the weekend. 'I'm sorry about calling so late,' she said, and sounded it. 'But our baby has come down with a cold, and we just can't leave him. Perhaps you have a vacancy later in the summer?'

Camryn said everything that was appropriate, and booked the room for a weekend in August. Then she put the telephone down and swore.

Cancellations were a part of the business; she had

always known that, and she planned around it. Still, it didn't happen often, and when it did it was an unpleasant shock; losing three nights' lodging in her most expensive room, and the afternoon tea as well, would put a nasty hole in her profits for the weekend. It wasn't likely that she'd get another call for the room on such short notice.

She glared across the kitchen at the rich chocolate cake that stood on the centre island, waiting to be iced with whipped cream and topped with cherries and nuts. She'd stayed up last night to bake it for this afternoon's tea because the young woman had told her that chocolate was her husband's favourite. Another wasted effort, she thought.

'Think positive,' she told herself. 'You can take Susan to the park for a while after all.'

And there was another bright spot as well, she realised. At least Patrick hadn't happened to be sitting in her kitchen this morning. He would no doubt have had a few choice things to say about the problems she would have if she counted on every reservation bringing in money. As it was, she thought, what Patrick didn't know couldn't hurt him.

After a quick romp in the park, Susan curled up with Ipswich and Freddy Bear on the solarium floor and fell asleep. Camryn covered her with a soft blanket and started to work on the light, puffy sweet rolls that would be the highlight of tomorrow's breakfast menu. They weren't hard to make, but they took time, and the afternoon crept towards evening while she worked. Susan was still asleep, and Sherry hadn't come home yet.

Darn the girl, Camryn thought. I told her quite clearly that she must be here tonight because people will be checking in. What's happened to her this week, anyway? I've never seen such irresponsible behaviour from her.

She heard a car pull up under the porte-cochère just as she took the last pan from the oven, and she heaved a sigh of relief. When the back doorbell rang, she was startled. Sherry must have her arms full, she thought, and hurried to help. Then she saw the masculine silhouette on the etched glass panel, and flung the door wide.

'Patrick!' she said, with a sort of squeak, as delight surged through her in a wave. She quickly smothered the feeling. Of course I'm happy to see him, she thought; I hated the idea of going to this affair completely on my own, not knowing anyone.

He was looking her over carefully, from her hair, tied back with a Paisley scarf, to her favourite old worn jeans, half-concealed by a pristine white apron. 'Surely that isn't what you're planning to wear to the picnic, Camryn?'

'Not the apron, no,' she flashed. 'What do you think I'd be likely to wear, Patrick?' Then she paused and inspected him through narrowed eyes. He was wearing a grey-beige linen sports jacket and dark trousers——

Camryn stepped back from the door and motioned him inside. Silently, she walked around him, studying the way his shoes gleamed, and how his carefully knotted Chinese-blue tie lay smoothly under the collar of his pale blue shirt.

It was a lot more casual than what he wore at the bank, but it was not the usual garb for a picnic—at least, not the sort Camryn was used to. And somehow she didn't think Patrick would be the one who was out of place.

She closed her eyes in pain. I might have known, she thought wildly. With my luck, this couldn't possibly be an ordinary picnic!

CHAPTER SIX

'You could at least have warned me that this picnic isn't the kind that involves hot dogs and ants,' she said bitterly.

'Didn't I?'

'Don't look innocent. I could have arrived in my tennis shorts and sandals and been——'

'A real hit?' he offered helpfully. His gaze dropped slowly down the length of her body. 'But not as much as if you were wearing a swimsuit.'

'Are you trying to sabotage me, McKenna?'

'Of course not. I'm here, aren't I?'

She swallowed the lump in her throat. It was hard to concentrate when the man was staring at her as if he was trying to remember the curves that her apron disguised.

Finally, almost reluctantly, he said, 'We really don't have time to argue about it, Camryn.'

'All right, I'll go change my clothes. You might as well come up.'

He bounded up the first flight of stairs after her. 'And help?'

Don't take it personally, Camryn, she warned herself. He doesn't mean anything. 'That wasn't what I had in mind, no. But you can sit in the solarium and be comfortable—it may take me a while to find something appropriate to wear.'

'I was afraid you meant something boring like that.' He sounded disgruntled.

On the solarium floor, Susan sat up and rubbed her

eyes. 'Is it time to get ready for the picnic?' she asked sleepily.

Camryn smothered a sigh and went over to kneel beside her daughter to give her a hug. 'I misunderstood, sweetheart,' she said. 'It's a different kind of picnic, and I'm afraid you can't go after all.'

The little face crinkled up, and Susan started to sob, noisy, wretched, miserable sounds that made it seem that her heart was breaking.

Patrick looked less than impressed. He sat down in a comfortable chair near the door.

Camryn was appalled. Of all the times to stage a scene. Susan, this isn't it, she wanted to say, but it would have done no good. 'She doesn't normally react like this,' she said. She pulled Susan on to her lap. 'It's just that she's still half-asleep——'

'She doesn't sound half-asleep to me. Camryn, we're going to be late. Go get dressed and let me deal with Susan.'

She eyed him warily, the sobbing child still in her arms. 'Look, Patrick, if Sherry doesn't get home I can't go anywhere, anyway. She must have forgotten——'

'Well, get dressed first, and we'll see. If she doesn't show up, we'll worry about it then.'

'I suppose you carry a list of baby-sitters in your wallet!'

At that horrible word, Susan cried even harder. Patrick got up, lifted her bodily out of Camryn's arms, and returned to his chair. He looked at Camryn and jerked a commanding thumb toward the stairs.

She stood up and put her hands on her hips. 'All right, if you're going to be a dictator. But don't you dare scold her for being upset. It's my fault, not hers. And yours, as well—you could have made it clear from the beginning that it wasn't a children's event!'

'Guilty as charged. So run along and let me do penance, all right?' He settled Susan more comfortably on his lap and stroked her hair. She turned her face into his shoulder, with a little hiccup, but for the moment she'd stopped wailing.

Camryn stood there and stared at him for another couple of moments before she turned towards the stairs. She thought she heard him mumur the words 'picnic' and 'games' and 'kids' before she was out of hearing range.

I wish him luck, she thought as she ran up the stairs. Susan didn't throw tantrums very often, but when she did they were generally prize-winners. Patrick had no idea what he was getting into. She only hoped that this time Susan would be reasonable. . .

Oh, why worry about it? she asked herself. What difference does it make whether he thinks Susan is the most obnoxious brat ever born? It wouldn't matter if he thought she was a perfect lady, either.

The tap at her bedroom door a few minutes later startled her, and she almost stuck her mascara brush into her eye. Sherry poked her head around the door. 'Patrick said I'd better come up and tell you I was home. Why? Did you think I'd forgotten?' She sounded irritated at the idea.

I certainly did, Camryn thought. But she's here now, and that's all that really matters, so why make a fuss? 'You're not normally so late. I was afraid something might have happened to you.'

'Not a chance,' Sherry muttered, and let the door drop shut behind her.

Camryn sat there staring at the door for a moment. Of

course, she thought. It's Friday night, and she's probably had to turn down a date. But it's the first time since she moved into the Stone House that she's ever made a fuss like that. . .

She would have liked to tiptoe back down to the solarium, to overhear what was going on. But sneaking down the wide oak staircase at the Stone House was impossible; too many of the steps creaked. Susan met her in the doorway.

'I get to go to a party tomorrow!' she crowed. 'With Patrick! A big party, with lots of kids and games and prizes and——'

Camryn shot a look at him. 'Penance?' she quoted drily.

He studied the apricot-coloured sun-dress that left her shoulders bare and nodded approvingly. 'It's my parents' Fourth of July party. I've asked Susan to be my date.'

'You shouldn't promise what you can't deliver.'

'I can deliver. There will be games and prizes and lots of kids.'

'Except for Susan, perhaps. I am running a business here, you know, and I can't just leave it at the drop of a hat——'

'If you insist, I suppose we could take a chaperon along,' he added arily. 'I wonder if Sherry would like to come?'

'I want Mommy,' Susan said.

Patrick shrugged. 'You heard her.'

'That's exactly what I mean,' Camryn accused. 'Getting her hopes up before you know if it's going to be possible——'

'Go on and have a good time, Camryn,' Sherry said. Camryn hadn't even seen her sitting in the corner window-seat till she spoke. 'I certainly don't have any plans for tomorrow.' She turned and stared out at the street again.

Camryn thought, For two cents I'd go and grab that girl and shake her till she tells me what's wrong. But Sherry was an adult, and if she didn't want to talk about it no one could force her. Camryn sighed. 'I suppose I'm ready to go,' she told Patrick.

He gave Susan a hug. 'See you in the morning,' he promised

'I wish you hadn't invited her,' Camryn said. She closed the back door carefully behind them and went out to the car. 'It's a family party, and she shouldn't be——'

'No, it's not. It's a block party that gets bigger every year. Last summer, half the university was there.' Patrick helped her into the car.

'You shouldn't invite her just because you feel guilty about tonight. You shouldn't attempt to buy her forgiveness by giving her something you originally had no intention of offering——'

Patrick leaned into the car. His hand cupped her chin and turned her face up to his. 'Be quiet,' he ordered, and kissed her.

Little flickers of electricity trembled along Camryn's veins. Her mouth softened under his, and his tongue slipped gently between her lips, seeking, testing, exploring. She made a little sound, and his hand slid to her throat, his fingertips resting softly on the pulse point below her ear as if he was searching for something. . .

He let her go, finally, just a couple of minutes short of the moment when her whole body would have slumped into a melting puddle against the soft upholstery. He walked around the car and slid behind the wheel, and Camryn thought hazily that apart from the fact that he was breathing a little faster then normal, he appeared to be perfectly fine. She, on the other hand, didn't feel normal at all.

She checked the mirror on the back of the sun-visor and sighed. Her lips were slightly swollen, and her eyes were huge and dark and moist. She reached for her tiny make-up kit. 'Now I've got to fix the damage. Why did you do that, anyway?' she asked briskly, trying to sound matter-of-fact.

'Don't you know?'

She darted a frightened look at him. He sounded serious. I can't handle this, she thought. I really can't.

He took one hand off the wheel and brushed the back of his fingers against her cheek, and murmured, with a smile, 'Because I think it's very sexy to watch a woman repair her lipstick, that's why.'

Dianna Stanford's idea of a picnic was more like a Buckingham Palace garden party. An entire section of Lakemont's largest park had been roped off, and a series of tents, all complete with wooden floors, had been erected to form a huge square.

I should have known, Camryn thought with a jaundiced look at her own flat-heeled shoes, that Dianna wouldn't let a little thing like grass interfere with fashion!

In one of the tents, space was set up for a band and a dance-floor. Another looked like a hive full of caterers' men, all scurrying around with quantities of food. The next tent was full of small tables, already set with napkins and flatware and glasses—not linen and silver and crystal, exactly, Camryn noted, but not paper and plastic, either.

In the next tent, a long bar was set up, and people were milling around with glasses in hand. It wasn't a big crowd, perhaps a hundred people altogether, but the noise level was already high.

'What would you like?' Patrick asked. 'There's champagne, or they can do any mixed drink you'd like, I'm sure. Or if you'd rather have something innocent——'

'At the last picnic I went to,' Camryn said thoughtfully, 'the beverage of the day was warm beer, because the hostess forgot the ice to pack it in. The alternative was dipping water out of Lake Michigan.'

Patrick shuddered. 'Champagne,' he decided, and went to get it.

Warren Stanford's booming voice said, 'Hello, my dear,' and he swooped down to put a dry kiss on Camryn's cheek.

He's been at the bar for a while, Camryn thought, or else he can't quite remember who I am, and he doesn't want to ignore me. I should be grateful; either way, it's less destructive than his handshake!

She smiled at him and said hello, and cast about for a topic of conversation. Be charming, Patrick had said, and she was willing to try. But before she could come up with a remark that was sufficiently captivating, an elderly lady in a pale blue spangled cocktail dress slipped between them. She put one hand on Camryn's arm, and one on Warren Stanford's.

'I just had to tell you,' she said, 'what a delightful young man your Patrick is. He's always so helpful, and so charming, and he has such a way about him.'

That's nice, Camryn thought. I'll have to tell him the matrons are complimenting him to his boss—just in case he doesn't already know it.

'You're an extremely lucky young woman, Mrs McKenna,' the lady said, with a melting smile at Camryn.

Patrick reached for her hand and put a cold glass into it. Camryn nearly dropped it. *Mrs McKenna?* she thought. Where had that come from?

The woman patted Camryn's hand, where her gold wedding band gleamed. 'You should hang on to him.'

Patrick smiled at the woman. 'Mrs McKenna?' he said thoughtfully. 'It's got a nice lilt to it, hasn't it, Mrs Johnson? My mother's gotten quite fond of it. She says she's only going to share it with very special ladies, and I haven't found anyone who meets her approval yet.'

Mrs Johnson looked disappointed. She pursed her lips and shook her head and turned away, and as soon as she was gone Warren Stanford laughed, and said, 'Very neat, my boy.'

Camryn tried to conceal a sigh of relief. Patrick smiled down at her. 'Drink your champagne,' he recommended.

As she raised her glass, she saw, out of the corner of her eye, Dianna Stanford, tall and slim and elegant in red silk. Her hand was resting on the arm of a very good-looking man with prematurely white hair, but Dianna was looking at Camryn, and the spite in her eyes was like a rock hitting Camryn in the face.

Patrick took her arm. 'Shall we wander around and mingle? It's my duty, you know.'

She said under her breath, 'Maybe you should tell Dianna that this is only business.'

He looked down at her thoughtfully. 'Maybe I don't want to,' he countered.

'Then I suggest you be on the lookout for arrows coming in your direction. I certainly am.'

'Don't worry about Dianna.'

'What's the matter with her, anyway?'

'Nothing much. Once upon a time, Dianna convinced

herself that I was going to ask her to marry me, and she hasn't quite forgiven me for never getting around to it.'

'Oh, in that case I can certainly see why you're not worried!'

'Is that sarcasm I hear dripping from your voice?'

'Haven't you ever heard about a woman scorned?'

'Who said she was scorned? I certainly didn't reject her—I just never proposed.' He watched the bubbles rise in his tulip glass, and added thoughtfully, 'I thought about it. I simply couldn't bring myself to do it.'

'Why not?' Camryn asked tartly. 'I'd think there would be lots of advantages for an aspiring young banker.'

His voice was a soft and wicked murmur. 'Because if this is a mere picnic, I'm terrified of what she would put together for a wedding reception.'

Camryn tried to smother a giggle, and choked on her champagne. Don't encourage him, she told herself. He's hopeless enough as it is!

'Besides, she's certainly got masculine company enough tonight without me,' he went on. 'That's the president of Lakemont's major industry, and if she's foolish enough to mess around with him, that only confirms my opinion.'

'Why?' Camryn stole a look at the man.

'Because he isn't completely divorced yet.'

'Maybe it's only business between him and Dianna, too. Like our partnership.'

'Perhaps it is. After his wife gets finished with him, he may need an infusion of cash.' He sipped his champagne. 'And if you say one more word about Dianna, I'm going to take you off to a secluded corner of the park and shut you up in the only way I've ever found that works.'

'Oh.' It was a bare squeak, as she remembered how

effective his methods had been earlier, when he hadn't wanted to talk any more about whether Susan should go to his parents' party. 'I'll be careful.'

He grinned, and a wicked sparkle lit his eyes. 'On second thoughts, don't,' he murmured. 'It sounds like a lot more fun than sitting through this damned picnic.'

It was a beautiful evening, and Camryn couldn't help but think that it would have been a perfect one for a real picnic—one that took place on a blanket with only the stairs for a roof, and only the infinite variations of cricket song for accompaniment. It was a relief when, a bare ten minutes after Warren Stanford left the dance-tent to the younger generation, Patrick said, 'Ready to go home?'

A relief, and a disappointment, too. The promptness of his suggestion made it very clear, Camryn thought a bit sadly, that he'd been thoroughly bored by the picnic, and probably by her company as well. At least, she thought, there was no need to carry it on through tomorrow, at his parents' party. She'd find a way to explain to Susan that she could not go

She told him that, as he drove her home. He didn't answer.

'It's a beautiful evening, isn't it?' she said finally. 'The full moon, and the stars.'

He nodded and parked the car beside the Stone House. 'Are you going in right away?'

Was that a hint not to bother to invite him in for coffee? 'No, I think I'll sit on the terrace for a while,' she said carelessly, 'and watch the moon.'

'May I join you?' Before she recovered her breath, he added, 'I live in one of those big apartment blocks downtown, so I don't have a terrace.'

'Besides, in the middle of the city, the moon looks like

just another streetlight,' Camryn agreed. She led the way to the secluded flagstone terrace behind the house.

He glanced at the furniture, and up at the moon. 'I think we'll have the best view from there, don't you?' He didn't wait for an answer, but led her over to a small, canvas-upholstered love-seat, just big enough for two, and settled her comfortably in it, with his arm around her and her head against her shoulder. His hand came to rest against the sensitive skin just under her ear, and his thumb idly stroked her earlobe.

They sat that way for long minutes, and Camryn found herself trying not to breathe for fear of disturbing the moment. She looked up at him through half-closed eyes. The soft moonlight caught in his eyelashes, and cast long shadows across his cheekbones.

It was a long time since she had sat this way with a man—a very long time indeed, she thought, remembering how seldom Mitch had been home at all in that last couple of years, much less with time just to sit and look at the moon.

There was something very restful about Patrick McKenna, she thought vaguely. Perhaps she'd been wrong, and he hadn't been bored tonight at all. In any case, she wasn't going to worry about it; it was very pleasant to sit here like this. . .

'Camryn,' Patrick said softly. 'I've got to ask you——'

She murmured something, a protest, perhaps, at having this quiet perfection interrupted.

'While you were married, did you like making love?'

Her eyes opened wide. She didn't pull away from him, but her whole body tensed warily. 'What on earth is this all about?'

'Don't jump up and run. I know the proposition from

your friend the doctor turned you off, and I can certainly see why. But was it just him? You sounded as if you found the whole idea of sleeping with someone nauseating.'

She closed her eyes again. 'No, it's not that. But I have to admit I don't see why so many people go crazy about it. Take my so-called friend the doctor, for example. He's got a perfectly good wife—why would he want me?'

He was silent for so long that she finally opened her eyes and looked up to see if he'd gone to sleep or something. Instead, he was staring at her, his eyes dark, with an expression in them that was almost incredulous. The way he looked at her did something funny to her insides, and her toes tried to curl themselves up into knots.

'You really don't know why?' His arm tightened around her, just a little. 'I'm tired of looking at the moon, Camryn,' he whispered. 'I'd much rather look at you instead. . .'

His first kiss was tender. Her lips softened automatically to meet his, and as she relaxed his mouth grew more possessive, wandering across the hollow of her cheek, caressing the soft line of her throat, then returning to her lips to plunder. He drew her even more closely against him, and after a few minutes she didn't know any longer where her body stopped and his began. She could feel his heart beating strongly against her breast—or was it her own heart instead?

His fingertips traced the soft skin of her shoulders, slipped under the edge of the sun-dress, then retreated to caress her breast. The heat of his hand seemed to dissolve the thin fabric. It sent a shudder of feeling through her, followed by a sharp pang of sanity. They were practically making love on the terrace. . . How utterly mad could she be?

'Let me go,' she whispered.

Frustration gave his voice a rough edge. 'I want to touch you, Camryn, every inch of you. I want to make love to you——'

'Please, Patrick.'

His breathing sounded harsh in the stillness, and for an instant she was almost afraid, but he let her go. She slipped slowly away from him, leaning back in the corner of the love-seat, uneasily aware that she wasn't far enough away from him to be safe, but knowing that she lacked the strength to move.

He ran a hand through his hair. She noticed, vaguely, that it was the first time she'd seen it really messed up. It looked good on him, and she raised a hand so she could weave her fingers through the dark waves; then she realised that it wouldn't be the smartest thing to do just now.

'Why are you pulling away, Camryn?' His voice held a harsh note. 'Because if you went to bed with me, you'd feel disloyal to Mitch?'

She shook her head. 'No. I don't think Mitch has anything to do with it.'

'Then would you mind telling me what the hell is going on? I feel as if I just got hit by a truck——'

'Would you like some coffee?'

He looked at her for a long moment, and then he smiled wryly. 'Coffee is your answer whenever you're feeling desperate, isn't it?' He stood up. 'No, thanks. I think I'd better go home instead. I'll see you tomorrow.'

'Patrick?'

'Yes?'

'I'm sorry.' It was a bare whisper.

'Well, that's some relief.' He opened the car door and leaned against it. 'Don't sleep well, Camryn.'

She didn't. She dreamed that she had gone to bed with him, and woke in the still coolness of dawn feeling exhausted, frustrated and horrified at herself. 'Just last week,' she lectured herself, 'you thought you'd probably never feel the desire to make love with anyone ever again. And now——' Just thinking about the vivid images her dreaming mind had conjured up brought hot colour flooding to her face.

Obviously, she thought, her physical side hadn't died after all. It had merely been in cold storage somewhere, waiting for a chance to attack her when it was least expected.

Which left her, very squarely, in the middle of a problem. She could hardly say she didn't find Patrick McKenna attractive, when she'd spent the best part of an hour last night in his arms. And now that her body seemed to have come to life again, she could scarcely spend the next twenty years taking cold showers, either.

But there was something deep inside her that shuddered away from the idea of having to explain to Susan why there was a man in her bedroom. . .

It had all been a great deal easier last week, she told herself. Perhaps what was happening to her now was a nightmare, she thought, without a great deal of hope. And perhaps, if she was very careful not to think about it, it would all go away.

Sherry arrived in the kitchen less than five minutes after Camryn and grabbed an apron. 'I'll take care of the breakfast-in-bed crowd,' she offered, and started taking trays out of the corner cabinet where they were always stacked.

Camryn stood stock-still for a full minute, staring at her, while Sherry briskly arranged baskets and china and flatware on the trays. She wanted to demand an explanation of Sherry's sudden transformation, but she thought that asking might send Sherry back into vagueness, and this morning she needed all the help she could get. So she turned her back and started the coffee perking instead, and put the trays of buns back into the oven to warm, and began to check items off her list of things to do.

'Sherry, can you pick up the laundry? I'll need the big tablecloth for tomorrow's breakfast buffet, and since you aren't busy today. . .' With all the confusion yesterday, she thought, it'll be a wonder if that's the only thing I forgot.

'Did I say I wouldn't be busy?' Sherry paused in the middle of filling a teapot, and looked across the room with a soft smile. 'Oh, yes, I remember it now. That was before I made plans.'

Susan danced in, singing an off-key little song. She hadn't combed her hair, but she was already wearing her best new pair of pink shorts and the matching flowered top, and she was carrying her sandals. 'Is Patrick here yet?' she demanded the moment she came in. 'I'm all ready for the party.'

Camryn's heart sank. I'm caught, she thought, between Susan's plans and Sherry's. If Sherry isn't going to be here, that means I have to be, and if Susan can't go to that damned party after all, last night's tantrum will look like a mere April shower beside the hurricane she'll create today. On the other hand, it would serve Patrick right if I stayed at home and let her go with him, she thought, and sighed. Susan would probably go, and that made her feel sadder yet.

'What plans, Sherry?' she demanded.

'I invited a guest for brunch, that's all. I didn't think you'd mind.'

Relief surged through Camryn. 'Of course I don't mind.'

'Well, don't let it interfere with your party. *Please.*' It was heartfelt. 'Go, and have a good time——'

Camryn laughed. 'And don't come back too soon, right? Don't worry, Susan and I will stay out of your way. Shall I phone before I come home to be sure the coast is clear?'

Sherry shook her head. 'No, it's just brunch. He finally called last night—I thought he was never going to. There's a note on your desk, by the way—I reserved a room for his mother at the end of August.'

'Your young man from the library? Why would he want a room for——?' She stopped abruptly.

Sherry was staring at her blankly. 'Him?' she said. 'You thought I was waiting for him to call? I meant John Marlow.'

Camryn closed her mouth with an effort, and then said, 'Lady Marlow is coming again? Sherry——'

'She's not bad, really, when you get to know her.' Sherry sounded a little doubtful, Camryn thought, but determined.

'And you're dating her son?'

'I wouldn't say that. One brunch does not a relationship make. But with any luck at all——'

'So that's why you were so willing to brave Mrs Marlow with breakfast last weekend?'

Sherry nodded. 'I thought for a while I was being a real moron,' she confided. 'He thought you were pretty wonderful, but he didn't seem to notice me at all. But on Saturday night when he brought his mother back and saw what a domestic soul I was, spending the evening playing games with Susan——'

'Having neatly gotten Susan's mother out of the way by sending her to the movies,' Camryn added drily.

'Well—you had a good time, didn't you?' Sherry was unrepentant.

'That's beside the point.'

'Not that it seemed to do any good—a whole week and he didn't even call me. But last night when he phoned for the reservation we talked a while, and then. . .'

'I get the picture. Sherry Abbott, you're a little schemer!'

Twin dimples flashed in Sherry's cheeks. 'Yes, I am,' she admitted. 'But then, if it's worth having, it's worth working for—isn't that what you always say?'

The doorbell rang, and Susan bounced up from the floor and danced off to answer it. She came back a couple of minutes later, one small hand tucked confidently into Patrick's, chattering. He was wearing tennis shorts and running shoes and a sweatshirt emblazoned with a university logo.

'You're early,' Camryn told him.

He stared admiringly at the trays of iced buns. Camryn put one on a plate and handed it across to him. He took a bite and said comfortably, 'And it paid off, too.'

'I see the dress-code is different today. Are you comfortable like that? I suppose you could ask the laundry to press a crease into your shorts——'

'Believe me, I'd be hooted out of the house if I did. Camryn, haven't you ever learned that the main rule of fashion is to fit into the surroundings?' He polished off the bun, licked his fingers, and looked hopefully at the tray.

'Help yourself—I'm not going to wait on you. Is your mother the kind of hostess who would be insulted if a guest brought extra food?'

'Depends. What are you bringing?'

Camryn pointed to the chocolate cake that was still sitting forlornly on the centre island. 'I have to put it together.'

'Who cares what Mom thinks? The rest of us will be humbly grateful.'

Sherry wailed. 'I was going to snitch a piece of that for my brunch——'

'And show John Marlow your culinary skills? Forget it. But I'll be happy to send Susan along on all your dates, if that would help.'

Sherry groaned. 'I know when I'm beaten.' She picked up a tray and went off down the hall with a dignified set to her shoulders.

Patrick started on his third bun. 'I have to keep up my energy,' he said when Camryn raised a questioning eyebrow. 'And since I didn't get any sleep last night— did you sleep well?'

'No.'

'Good. You deserved it.'

But she thought that he looked a bit startled that she had actually admitted it. As far as that went, she had to confess, she was a little surprised that she'd said it, herself.

CHAPTER SEVEN

THERE was no doubt about where the party was being held; it could be heard from two streets away. 'That's why they made it a block party,' Patrick explained. 'It's easier to invite the neighbours than it is to keep the noise down.'

He nosed the car carefully down a narrow driveway beside a tall old Queen Anne house and through a hotch-potch of people who were milling around the back yard. The house itself looked as if it was breaking out with multi-coloured measles; at various spots, paint had been splashed on seemingly at random, in a rainbow of colours. But the house looked solid and well-kept; the porches were sturdy, the roofline was straight and even, and the octagonal tower at one corner stood proudly against the summer sky, without a shingle missing from its elaborate siding. Camryn kept an eye out for paint cans and drop cloths, but she concluded by the time they reached the house that Kathleen McKenna had been talked out of her plan to turn the party into a house-painting session.

'What colour is it really going to be?' she asked.

'The house? Pink and grey and burgundy, I think—sounds horrible, doesn't it?'

Dennis McKenna met them at the door. 'Patrick, you can bring this young lady any time,' he said with a grin, relieving Camryn of the cake-stand. 'Glad you could come, Camryn, with or without the cake.'

'Thank you, Mr McKenna.'

He shook his head. 'Call me Dennis,' he said. 'When you say "Mr McKenna" around here, you're likely to draw a crowd.'

'Actually,' Patrick said, straight-faced, 'he's Dr McKenna. If you really want to make him feel that he stands out from the teeming masses, use that. It used to work very well for us kids when we were on the receiving end of a discussion of homework or chores——'

'Medicine?' Camryn asked Dennis.

'No—mathematics, at the university. And feel free to ignore Patrick; the rest of us do.' He set the cake aside and dropped to one knee. 'You must be Susan.'

The child nodded shyly and clung to her mother's hand, wary of all the confusion. But it wasn't for nothing that Dennis McKenna had raised a family of five; within minutes, he and Susan were fast friends and had gone off to watch the volleyball tournament in the back yard.

'I see that I wasn't necessary after all,' Camryn said as the man and the child went out of sight. She was half-serious; she was only beginning to realise how much Susan was growing up.

Patrick grinned. 'Of course we don't need you. I only brought you so you wouldn't throw a tantrum at being left out.' He grabbed her hand. 'Come and meet my grandmother.'

She must have looked startled. She had a sudden mental picture of a tiny old lady with white hair and a lace cap, rocking gently on the front porch and conducting a soft-voiced inquisition over her tatting.

Don't be a fool, Camryn warned herself. Even the fondest grandparent doesn't start investigations of her grandson's casual friends. He just doesn't want her to feel left out.

'We shouldn't have let Dad steal Susan, but I guess it

will be all right. My grandmother likes to meet the parents of my dates, too,' Patrick murmured.

Camryn jabbed him in the ribs. He jumped and looked wounded.

The Queen Anne house had a rambling floor plan, and he led her by the hand through most of the ground level. In the dining-room, Kathleen McKenna was supervising the placement of what looked like tons of food, in randomly assorted containers, on the big table. She smiled absently at Camryn and turned back to the job at hand.

My presence here is nothing so out of the ordinary, Camryn told herself. After all, last weekend Kathleen told Patrick to bring his friends. I like the feeling of being accepted as Patrick's friend, without questions. . .

The front hall was panelled with a lovely, mellow old wood. The house had been well-maintained, but here and there it showed the inevitable marks of family occupation. There were scratches and nicks and dents. She found herself wondering which of them Patrick was responsible for. Had he been the one who had roller-skated down the front hall? That was certainly what it looked like, from the scratches on the hardwood floor.

'Did you grow up here?' she asked.

'Didn't you see the historical marker at the end of the driveway, marking it as my first home?'

'A brass plaque, you mean? No, I missed that,' Camryn said drily.

'Actually, it's only my tiny footprints in concrete, made when they poured the new driveway. My mother figured if the stars in Hollywood could do it——'

'The footprints may be tiny,' Camryn said to no one in particular, 'but I'll bet the ego was already inflated.'

'I'll have you know that I was such an adorable child

that my parents had four more. That in itself is quite a recommendation, if you think about it.' He held the front door open. The centre panel was a pane of glass elaborately etched with a pineapple design.

Camryn ran a gentle finger across it. 'Lovely,' she said.

'Thank you. I picked it out myself, and bought it with my lawn-mowing money, the summer I slipped and threw a boomerang through the original one.'

'You should have been shot.'

'Why? Even my mother says this one's nicer.'

There was no old lady tatting in a rocking-chair on the front porch. There was no one there at all, in fact, despite the lines of chairs pulled up invitingly.

Most of the front lawn looked vaguely like an abandoned sand trap which had started to sprout unwanted growth, but along one side of the central walk an area had been roped off and carefully seeded, and here and there small tufts of grass were growing.

'Looks awful, doesn't it?' Patrick said. 'My father always wanted an elegant green lawn, but as the years went on the bare spots just kept getting bigger. He thought he had it made when we grew up, but he still can't keep the neighbourhood kids from walking on his grass. There they are.'

Off to one side of the lawn Camryn saw a group of adults. Patrick took the porch steps with a leap and started towards them.

'Patrick, don't you dare ruin my throw,' one of them said sharply, and he paused, holding Camryn back, while a horseshoe spun lightly through the air across the lawn and rang triumphantly as it settled around the stake.

'Between the neighbourhood kids and the senior citizens,' he murmured, 'it's no wonder Dad's ready to give up the idea of ever having grass.' He raised his voice. 'Here she is, Nell, and don't tell me you didn't notice. I saw you eyeing her when we came in the driveway.'

The woman who had thrown the ringer dusted off her hands and turned. She was nearly as tall as Patrick, and solidly built, with flyaway grey hair and deep lines in her face that spoke of humour as well as pain. She was wearing blue jeans that displayed a label any teenager would have approved of, and a red T-shirt emblazoned with a slightly rude phrase.

This is his grandmother? Camryn thought weakly as Patrick introduced her, and she shook Nell McKenna's hand. Her own was trembling a little as she looked up into dark blue eyes—the same shade as Patrick's eyes. . .

'Do you play horseshoes, my dear?' Nell McKenna's voice was low and had the texture of gravel.

'No, I'm afraid not.'

'You should. Wonderful exercise—it would build up those arm muscles. You young people are all out of condition.'

'Nell played softball till she was seventy-two,' Patrick said. 'She says she only stopped then because her doctor forced her to——'

'The arthritis in my shoulder,' Nell said. 'It was messing up my pitching arm.'

'It's certainly true that her earned-run average was creeping steadily upwards,' Patrick mused. 'But I don't think it had anything to do with the arthritis. We were just beating her.'

Nell put her hands on her hips and stared at him with her eyes narrowed. Then she turned to Camryn. 'Don't you think those shorts are indecent? Running around with bare legs like that!'

Camryn blinked at the sudden attack. Her shorts weren't skin-tight, or cut particularly high on the thigh, and judging by the T-shirt Nell didn't seem the prudish sort. Besides, those jeans she was wearing were pretty snug——

'Oh, not yours, Camryn,' Nell went on. 'I'd wear shorts myself if I still had legs like yours. I was referring to my grandson's hairy knees. They're offensive to look at.'

Patrick grinned. 'If you're trying to tell me to get lost so you can talk to Camryn, all you have to do is ask nicely, Nell.'

'And say *pretty-please*?' She snorted. 'Show some respect for your elders, Patrick, and go away. Come to think of it, if you'd really like to improve your standing with me, go talk some sense into your mother. This whole house-painting project of hers will be the death of me yet.'

'Nothing could be the death of you, Nell. You'll outlive us all.'

Nell ignored him. 'Now she wants to paint the whole inside, too. Says it makes sense to do it all at once, while the painters are here.'

Patrick shrugged. 'At least she's not expecting all of us to be the painters.'

'Who cares? It doesn't matter to me who applies the paint; the smell of it still give me splitting headaches. And if that's not enough, the colours she's going to use——'

'I'll mention it to her,' Patrick said callously. 'But you can't expect any of us to take you seriously, Nell. What happened to your philosophy of clean living and exercise preventing all health problems?'

'I'm not sick, I'm just allergic,' Nell called after him. 'If Kathleen had any compassion at all. . .' She turned to Camryn and smiled. 'Now that we're rid of him——'

'Your turn, Nell,' one of the other players interrupted, and Nell took a moment and threw another ringer.

'That's all the lessons you're getting today, fellas.' She drew Camryn off across the lawn. 'Besides,' she added with a smile, 'I want to be closer to the house when the stampede for the food begins. Does the little person I saw in the back of Patrick's car belong to you?'

'Yes. My daughter Susan.'

Nell's eyes were bright, and as inquisitive as a sparrow's. 'Divorced? Or never married?'

'Neither,' Camryn said tautly. 'Widowed.'

'You don't wear a ring.'

Camryn looked at the bare spot on her finger. Her hands were clenched together, and they were shaking with irritation at Nell McKenna, and at herself for being such a fool. She'd spent more time thinking about that ring this morning than the rest of her outfit and, after a lot of thought, she'd tugged the gold band off her finger and left it in her jewellery case, thinking that anything would be better than a repeat of last night's mistaken identity. Well, she'd obviously been wrong. 'I can't see what difference it makes,' she muttered.

'It doesn't.' Nell said without a second's hesitation. 'Just my busy-body instincts.'

'Besides, you don't wear a ring, either, and no one is implying that you've never been married.'

Nell chuckled. It was a low rumble, like thunder in the distance. 'Fair enough. Shall I take you around and introduce you to all the evidence?'

* * *

It took Camryn most of the day to sort the rest of the McKennas out of the crowd, because Nell's whirlwind tour of introductions was interrupted by lunch, which Nell direly referred to as a restaging of the plague of the locusts.

She was sitting on the edge of the back porch at mid-afternoon, with Susan taking an enforced break with her head in Camryn's lap, when a young man came to sit beside her, clutching a paper plate that held a huge wedge of her chocolate cake.

'I'm Patrick's little brother Colin,' he said with a sunny smile.

'I thought you might be. There's a family resemblanc,' she said, straight-faced. She didn't tell him that it wasn't dark hair and blue eyes so much as the size of the piece of cake that had told her they were related. It's not fair, she thought. Not a one of them displays an excess ounce of flesh.

'*Little brother* is merely a chronological term, of course,' Colin went on. 'I'm younger, but I'm three inches taller than he is, and he resents it. Anyway, I decided I should scrape an acquaintance with the pastry chef.' He dug his fork into the confection.

'Shouldn't you wait till you've tasted the cake? It would be awfully embarrassing to have to sit here beside me and eat it all if you don't like it.'

He grinned. 'I took that precaution a long time ago. This is my third slice. To tell the truth, I've had this one hidden in the butler's pantry behind the cans of spinach for a couple of hours, so nobody would get it away from me. Are you going to marry Patrick?'

She was watching Patrick just then; he was playing three-on-three basketball in the driveway, and at that instant he leaped to intercept a pass and went down on the asphalt. She jumped, involuntarily, as if it had been she who fell, and Susan stirred with a sleepy protest. Camryn's hand smoothed the child's hair and then relaxed as Patrick rolled to his feet with a laugh and plunged back into the game.

What a different side of him she had seen today, she thought. The well-groomed banker had vanished hours ago, submerged in the young man whose only goal seemed to be having a good time on a hot holiday afternoon. . .

And she thought, marry Patrick? I wouldn't mind marrying his whole family. . .

The idea came as a bit of a shock. I hadn't realised, she thought, just how lonely I'd let myself become. 'Why do you ask?' she said crisply.

Colin grinned and gestured with his fork. 'I just wanted to know if I could rely on one of your cakes at every future family gathering.'

'Don't count on it.'

'That's a shame.' He sounded genuinely sorry—but only for the sake of his appetite, Camryn thought.

Across the yard, Dennis McKenna blew a whistle and announced the start of a three-legged race. Susan sat up and rubbed her eyes sleepily and called Patrick's name; he broke away from the basketball game and came over. 'Do you want to be my partner?' he asked her, and his hand brushed against Camryn's bare leg as he lifted the child off the porch. He smiled at Camryn and carried Susan off across the yard.

Camryn's heart did a tiny little flip and settled uncertainly back into place. That was new, she admitted reluctantly. Darn Colin, anyway, for suggesting such a thing.

He polished off the last bite of cake. 'Camryn, if everything you make is this good, I'm going to start coming over for all my meals. What's the address of that place of yours?'

'Sorry, but I just do breakfast. And only for overnight guests, at that.'

He looked disgruntled. 'You're losing out on a sure bet, you know. A restaurant serving that kind of food—you could make your fortune. What's it called? The Stone House? I've even got a slogan for you. "Where the pastry is tender, and the house is rock-solid."'

The idea struck her fancy. She sat there and watched the breathless progress of the three-legged race, and thought about it. Why hadn't she thought of it before? She couldn't manage a fully fledged restaurant, of course, but surely she could work out a simple, limited luncheon menu, to be served by reservation only. And she had always loved doing the baking and fussing that went along with afternoon tea, and no one else in the city was offering a service like that. Why not do it every day—not just for her overnight guests, but for the public? Judging by Colin's reaction, there might be a demand. . .

And with the extra income—she couldn't wait to see if Patrick thought it would be enough to get her mortgage.

He dropped down beside her with a smile. 'We lost,' he said, and lay back flat against the porch. 'Susan went off to fill water balloons with the rest of the kids. She's learning all kinds of new games today.'

Camryn shuddered.

Nell pulled up a rocking-chair on the porch. 'I don't suppose you've talked to your mother yet, Patrick.'

'As a matter of fact, I have.' Patrick didn't open his

eyes. 'Give it up, Nell. Frankly, the place needs a coat of paint, inside and out. Besides, you've lived with Mother for fifteen years, and you ought to realise by now that once she's got the bug to do something she won't rest till it's done.'

'That's true enough,' Colin agreed.

'Why don't you just let her get the paint out of her system. You know that once it's finished, she'll forget all about it. She won't do so much as move a stick of furniture again for five years.'

'Furniture-moving doesn't give me headaches,' Nell said sternly. 'And if I have to smell paint for days and nights on end, I won't be alive to care in five years. I probably won't be alive in five days——'

'So check into a hotel.' Patrick didn't sound interested. 'Better yet, go and stay with Camryn for a week or two. You'll have all the comforts of home, with breakfast thrown in. You can find room for one irascible old lady, can't you, Camryn?'

'That's my favourite kind,' she murmured.

A smile tugged at the corner of his mouth, but he only said, 'I'll tell Mother the painters can come on Monday, then. It's all settled.'

Nell said tartly, 'That's easy for you to say. Who's paying for this, I'd like to know? You? You aren't expecting Camryn to do it for nothing, I hope——'

'What about for love? That's a charming idea,' Patrick said, with his eyes still closed.

Camryn tried to keep herself from turning red, and failed. 'I'm sure we can arrange a weekly rate.'

Patrick opened his eyes and considered her. 'I'll trust you,' he said finally. 'Send me the bill. We'll call it your birthday present, Nell. And Mother's, too,' he added under his breath.

Colin said, hopefully, 'As long as you're handing out money, Patrick, I'm having a little trouble making my car payments——'

'See me at the bank on Monday.'

Colin groaned. 'I knew it was too good to last.'

Nell stood up. 'I think I'll go and do a little packing. Oh, and Patrick, dear? I'll do my best to enjoy myself. It would be such a shame if I didn't get your money's worth.'

After the party broke up at twilight, they went down to the wide green-belt park on the shore of Lake Michigan to watch the city fireworks display over the lake. Patrick spread a blanket on the sand, and Susan, who was flat-out exhausted from her day, flopped down on it and went straight to sleep. She flinched a bit when the aerial bombs started going off, and she sat up and blinked at a few of the sky-rockets. 'Pretty,' she said when one huge golden burst lit the sky with spangles, and then went back to sleep with her head on Patrick's knee.

'This is the stuff nightmares are made off,' he mused.

'All the noise sinking into her subconscious mind?'

'Actually, I wasn't thinking about Susan's nightmares at all—just mine. I was watching you, in the glow of the fireworks, and thinking what a rotten shame it is that if I move, I'll wake her up.'

'It is?'

'Yes. As it is, I can't even reach you and drag you over here and kiss you.'

'Oh.' She didn't look at him.

'Has anyone ever told you what a beautiful profile you've got?' His voice was soft and husky, and it sent shivers down Camryn's spine. He had a knack for doing that, she thought, for giving an ordinary compliment a

twist that made it soft and appealing and oh, so seductive
to listen to. If he ever talked to Dianna Stanford like
this, she thought, I can understand why she feels the
way she does. How easy it would be to convince myself
that he means more than he says. How easy it is to love
him——

Above her head, a sky-rocket splintered into green
fragments; each bit fell screaming towards earth and
then, in rapid succession, burst into liquid golden fire.
But the explosion in the sky was no less shattering than
the one in Camryn's heart.

I love him. She tried it out hesitantly, in her mind,
feeling as if she were screaming the words. *I've fallen in
love with him.* . .

Out of the corner of her eye she studied him covertly,
as he watched the fireworks. She wanted to creep over
next to him and let him hold her, kiss her—do whatever
he wanted. And then, she admitted quietly, I want to go
home with him, for always.

It's too short a time, she told herself. You've only
known him a matter of days. And yet she was more sure
of herself than she had ever been before. A month from
now, a year, a decade—it wouldn't matter. She would
still be in love with Patrick McKenna.

And what about Patrick? That was a good question,
she thought. He had told her last night that he wanted
to make love, but he had said nothing about loving her.
He had taken her out to his parents' home today, but
was that only because he'd promised Susan the day, to
avoid the consequences of last night's tantrum? And
what about Susan? He was sitting there so still right now
in order not to disturb her rest, but what did that really
mean? A man could like a child, and enjoy her company,

and be entertained by her, without wanting to have her around on a regular basis.

And when a woman has a four-year-old child, she thought drearily, then any relationship certainly has to include both of them, or it can go nowhere at all.

She closed her eyes and let her mind drift, dreaming of what could be. The three of them, together, at the Stone House. . .Susan and Patrick, all dressed up for a Dads-and-Daughters banquet at school. . . Herself and Patrick, snuggling by the fire on a cold winter's night. . .

Don't be a fool, Camryn, she told herself. He's gone above and beyond duty in trying to fix your mortgage. And he certainly seems to enjoy your company, too. But don't ruin it by demanding more. Don't try so hard to figure out how the sky-rockets work that you let one of them explode in your face!

And perhaps, given some time—it had, after all, been such a little time. Once the mortgage was taken care of, then perhaps she could see what she really meant to him.

The mortgage. It reminded her that she needed to talk to him about it. 'Patrick?' she said. Her voice didn't want to work quite right.

'Hmm?' He sounded half-asleep.

She told him about Colin's careless comment, and the train of thought it had sparked for her.

'A restaurant?' he said doubtfully.

'Not really. A—sort of a private party service,' she explained. 'Reservations only, of course. I couldn't possibly manage big groups, and the varying crowd of a regular restaurant would drive me out of business in a week. But there aren't many nice places to have lunch in Lakemont. Surely businessmen would like a truly private place to entertain clients? And no one does afternoon tea the way I can—I could make a regular business out of hosting bridal showers and engagement parties and all that sort of thing. I don't know why I never thought of it before.'

'It had become dark, and in the interval between sky-rockets she couldn't see his face, only the dim silhouette of his body. 'Camryn, is that what you want to do for the rest of your life?' he asked quietly.

She drew her feet up and wrapped her arms around her knees and thought about it very seriously. Was it what she wanted? Could she even manage to do it? It would mean planning, and self-promotion, and months of hard work before she even knew if she would be successful. But wasn't the end worth the means?

'I'm not afraid of work, Patrick. And it's a way to get some extra money together, and trim the mortgage down.'

'You can't run a restaurant and go to college. It will be a lot different from what you're doing now.'

'Yes, it will. But if I like what I'm doing, maybe finishing my degree isn't so important after all. I can't manage going to college right now, that's for sure, so why not do this instead?'

He didn't answer, but he looked doubtful.

'Don't you think I can do it?'

There was a long silence. Then he said, very quietly, 'I think you can do whatever you make up your mind to do.'

It warmed her heart to know that he had confidence in her after all, and it gave her courage to go on.

'It's going to take a while to get it put together,' she said. 'And even longer to make a profit. In the meantime, I still have to do something about the mortgage.'

She clenched her fists and took a firm grip on her

courage. 'With the promise of extra income, surely I'm a better risk?' she began. 'And you said that if I had someone to guarantee my loan, that it would be a great deal easier to get. Maybe now, that person wouldn't even have to put up any money, just be a sort of character witness—a promise that I'll pay it back.'

'Something like that,' he said. 'But—'

'Will you back my loan, Patrick? Personally, I mean—not as a bank officer?'

She knew, in her heart, that she was really asking a great deal more than that. She was asking him to promise that there was something in the future for them, whatever it might be, for if he was willing to take this chance on her, then it must mean that he did not intend to turn his back on her.

He sighed heavily, and her heart slid to her toes and stayed there. 'I can't, Camryn.'

'But it isn't going to matter!' she said wildly. 'You won't have to come up with the money—I'm going to pay it back, I swear it! Dammit, Patrick, just a minute ago you said you had confidence in me! What happened to that?'

'Nothing happened. But there are regulations, honey. Me guaranteeing a loan for you is the sort of thing that gives bank examiners nervous tics. They'd be down on me in a matter of days. . .'

She lay back on the blanket and put her arm over her eyes. 'Maybe I should have taken the doctor up on his offer, after all,' she said drearily.

'Oh, if you're agreeable to that sort of arrangement, to hell with the bank examiners!' It was cheerful, and an instant later he said, 'I'm sorry, Camryn. That just popped out.'

She stood up stiffly. 'It's time to go home. The fireworks are over.'

He was silent for a long moment, then he shifted Susan's weight and freed himself and stooped to pick her up. 'We'll take this scheme to Warren first thing next week,' he said, 'and see what he thinks. The additional income will make it much easier for him to bend the rules—you may not even need a guarantee.'

For an instant, she didn't even really hear what he had said. Then she asked herself, Could this really be the end of it? Could the answer have been so simple after all?

Simple—well, it was hardly that, she thought. It was going to take a lot of hard work, and a lot of time. And the weight still rested squarely on her own two shoulders——Where it has always been, she reminded herself. That hasn't changed at all.

It was a quiet ride back to the Stone House. At the back door Camryn tried to rouse Susan, who muttered sleepily and refused to budge. Patrick lifted her bodily out of the back of the car. 'She's dead weight,' he warned Camryn. 'Would you like me to carry her up to bed?'

'Please.' She hadn't been looking forward to climbing those long flights of stairs with Susan in her arms.

It was the first time he had come upstairs with her, she thought as she led the way, and, though there really was no reason to be nervous, her heart was beating a tattoo rhythm. She turned on the night-light in Susan's room and watched as Patrick put the child carefully down on her bed. Camryn pulled her sandals off and decided to forget the rest; Susan's jersey shorts and shirt were very much like pyjamas, anyway. She tucked

Freddy Bear into the curve of the child's arm and gave her a gentle kiss.

Neither of them spoke till they were back downstairs. Patrick kissed her, almost casually—just a brush of his lips against her cheek. 'Goodnight,' he said.

'It isn't really late. Would you like coffee?'

He half-smiled, and Camryn remembered the night before, and the moonlight, and her offer, and started to turn red.

'I don't think it would be wise.'

'Why not?' Then she caught herself. 'I mean—of course. You don't have to explain.'

He smiled, a little ruefully, but his voice was deadly serious as he said, 'But I think I should. It's because there are too many things I want tonight besides coffee, Camryn. And because I don't want you to think I'm the same sort as your doctor friend.' He pulled his car keys from his pocket and turned towards the door.

She stood very still in the centre of the hall, knowing that if she stayed silent for one more instant the decision would be out of her hands, and he would not blame her. And then she knew that she couldn't do that. She could not let him leave.

Whatever else happened, whatever the future held, she wanted him—needed him—too much to let him go tonight.

Her fingers raised almost of their own will to touch the spot on her cheek where his lips had rested. 'Patrick. . .'

He turned, with his hand on the knob of the half-open door.

Her voice was little more than a whisper. 'It never occurred to me to think that you were like him. I just knew that you couldn't be. Please, I wish you'd come back inside. . .'

His eyes were dark. 'If I do, Camryn,' he said levelly, 'I may not leave.'

'I know.' It was only a whisper. 'Don't you see, Patrick? I don't want you to leave.'

CHAPTER EIGHT

THE weight of the world seemed to hang in the balance for a timeless instant, and then Patrick closed the door, and twisted the lock, and turned to face her.

For a second, Camryn felt panic percolate through her. I'm crazy, she thought. My hormones are raging out of control, as if I were seventeen again. . .

But that wasn't it, she knew. What she felt for him was not just a matter of a woman's physical longings suddenly come back to life. If that had been the case, she might have assuaged her hunger easily enough; there were no doubt plenty of men who would be willing, even eager, to take her to bed, if she chose to look for them. But none of those men could be Patrick, and only Patrick could soothe the need she felt tonight.

So, when he crossed the hall to her, she firmly put her fears behind her and held out her hands to him.

Her bedroom was dim, except where the ruffled white curtains let the moonlight filter in to throw shadowy patterns against the ceiling and over the quilt. The room was full of odd nooks and angles, because it had been fitted under the slant of the roof at the very top of the house. It wasn't particularly neat, either; she had made her bed this morning, but there were books and papers strewn around, and her dressing-table was a mess. Camryn looked around uncertainly in the dim light. It didn't seem the same place at all, seeing it for the first time through a man's eyes. What would he think of it—and her?

He seemed to catch her thoughts. 'Roses trailing over the wallpaper,' he murmured, 'and ruffles, and you, as I've dreamed of you. Camryn. . .'

She turned into his arms, and knew as she felt the solid warmth of him against her body that this was where she wanted always to remain.

Don't ask for always, she warned herself. You have tonight. No one can take that from you. Hold on to this one night with both hands, and treasure it forever.

She put all the longing she felt into their first kiss. She raised herself on her toes and leaned against him, her body tightly pressed against his, trusting him to support her. His heart was pounding; she could feel its rhythm against her breasts as he steadied himself to balance her weight. His hands slipped over the soft skin of her back—just when, she wondered, had he pulled her blouse free from the waistband of her shorts? He unerringly freed the fastener of her bra, and then his palms settled warmly on her ribs, holding her securely against him and at the same time allowing his thumbs to slide under the bra to caress the silky curve of her breasts.

'That's not very comfortable,' she whispered. 'It binds——'

'Is that an invitation to finish undressing you?' He didn't wait for an answer before disposing of her blouse and the offending bra, and as his hands closed softly over her taut breasts Camryn made a little noise, deep in her throat, that sounded like satisfaction. . .

His tongue probed caressingly, setting off tiny bursts of pleasure. He wasn't breathing quite steadily, she noted with idle concern. Her hands slipped slowly up his arms, over his shoulders, and tangled in his hair. The dark waves were softer than she had expected. She wanted to bury her face in his hair, to breathe the scent of him, to drown herself in sensation.

She pushed herself a little way from him—it took a great deal of effort—and tugged his shirt free so she could slip her hands under it. She let her fingers skim over his chest and down to tug at the fastener of his shorts, and opened her eyes in innocent surprise as he groaned.

'Camryn, you're driving me to the brink,' he said hoarsely.

'But I haven't even started yet,' she whispered.

He said something under his breath, then picked her up and deposited her on the bed. His hands were almost impersonal as he disposed of the rest of her clothes and his, and his breathing had slowed almost to normal by the time he joined her there and lay, not touching her, just looking at her in the moonlight.

We can't have that, she thought. She ran her fingernails gently down his spine and back up again.

He smiled lazily at her. 'Impatient?' he asked softly. 'I've half a mind to make you wait, just to show you who's in charge here——'

She locked her hands together at the back of his neck and pulled him down to meet her lips, willing and warm and eager.

'Some other time,' he whispered, and then the storm broke around them.

Their passion was a hurricane of desire that spun wildly out of control, carrying them madly upwards into a spiralling maelstrom of feeling that seemed to have no beginning and no end. Eventually it tossed them back to earth, like the shattered survivors of a shipwreck flung up on to the beach of an unmapped island, and they clung together as the storm abated, as breathing slowed and hearts returned to normal. . .

Normal? Camryn thought dizzily. As if, after that, anything could ever be normal again!

Eventually, Patrick shifted her more comfortably in his arms and turned his face into her neck, with his lips pressed against the soft skin just under her ear. 'What are you muttering about?' he asked indistinctly, as she made a sleepy little protest.

The fact that you moved, she thought. Perhaps if I close my eyes and concentrate and am very careful not to breathe, we can lie here together forever. . . She tried to ignore the slow, sensual circles he was drawing around her navel with one gentle fingertip.

'You don't wear white boxer shorts, after all,' she murmured, only half-aware of what she was saying. She was so very tired.

His smile gleamed in the moonlight. 'I didn't know I was supposed to.'

'I'll bet it's in the bank's dress-code.' She yawned.

He captured her hand and held it against his chest. 'Do you spend a lot of time wondering about my underwear?'

'That's only an example. In fact, McKenna, you're a disservice to the stodgy image of bankers all the way around.' But it was a sleepy murmur, and some of the words came out sounding funny.

'I'm doing my best,' he whispered. 'If you want stodgy, Camryn——'

She slipped even closer to him, burying her nose against his shoulder and flinging her arm over his chest as if to hold him next to her.

'Then I guess I'll just lie here and hold you while you

have a nap,' he said wryly. She heard him, vaguely, but she was already sliding down the long incline into sleep.

A long time later she stirred and flung out a hand, and found him gone. She closed her eyes again, trying to remember. It was real, she told herself frantically. He was here; I couldn't have produced all that from nothing more than desire and imagination. . .

Something stirred across the room, and she sat up, clutching the sheet to her breasts. A shadow detached itself from the night; now that the moonlight was no longer oozing through the windows, the corners of the room were gloomy. The shadow was reaching for something on the floor.

'Patrick! I thought——' There was surprise in her voice.

He stood up. It must have been the act of his leaving her bed that had roused her, she thought; he hadn't even started to dress.

'Did you think that I was Mitch?' he said softly.

'No.' It was only a whisper. I thought that you were a dream come true, she wanted to say. 'Where are you going?'

'Home. I thought you'd prefer it if I cleared out before daylight—considering your guests, and all.'

And Susan, she thought, with sudden gratitude for his understanding. But tonight is mine, she thought. And it's still tonight. . . She lay back against the pillows. 'There's plenty of time, Patrick. Come back to bed.'

'Camryn, it's almost dawn. You're too nearly asleep to know what you're saying.'

She shook her head. 'I'm not too sleepy to know I want you,' she admitted.

'Believe me, it breaks my heart to argue with you, when it would be to my advantage to be agreeable.'

She smiled up at him and patted the pillow beside her. 'So stop talking and come back to bed and be agreeable,' she invited softly.

He hesitated for an instant, and then picked up his clothes and began to get dressed, quietly and methodically. She sat up, staring at him. Didn't he want her any more? Had the beauty she had seen last night passed him by?

Or was he anxious to be gone for fear that she might expect commitment if he stayed? Was he afraid of what she would demand if Susan was to find them there together?

Her eyes focused on the old alarm clock on the bedside table. He was right about the time, she thought. It was almost dawn, nearing the hour when the world would begin to stir once more. It made her feel a little better to know that he had stayed with her as long as he dared. But she was a bit angry with herself, too. She had wasted her precious night, going to sleep in his arms like that——

No, she thought. That wasn't a waste, exactly. But I wish I had stayed awake instead, so I had every moment to remember. . .

He sat down on the bench beside her dressing-table to put on his shoes, and when he stood up again she pushed back the blankets.

'Don't get out of bed,' he said, a little sharply. 'I can't handle it.' He didn't kiss her, only leaned over the bed to brush his knuckles across her cheek and against the glossy brown hair that spilled over her pillow. She reached up to cup her palm along his stubbly jaw, and he pulled back as if he'd been burned by the sudden heat that sprang up between them. Then, with a twisted smile, he slipped out of her room and down the stairs.

She heard a step or two squeak, but only because she was straining her ears for the sound. He was being very careful, she thought.

And then she pulled her pillow around and buried her face in it and cried herself back to sleep because he had left her there alone.

She didn't wake till late and had to rush madly about to get the breakfast buffet set up in time. To top off her irritation, she discovered that Sherry had forgotten to stop at the laundry yesterday after all, and so Camryn had to improvise a covering for the big dining-room table.

She was too absorbed in John Marlow yesterday to think about business, Camryn thought sharply, and then reminded herself that much the same thing had been happening to her. If she hadn't gone to that picnic yesterday, or if she had come home last night instead of going to the fireworks display——

She stopped for a minute in the middle of her kitchen, a small, secret smile curving her mouth. No, she really couldn't blame Sherry, not when she herself was perfectly willing to work twice as hard today rather than to have sacrificed last night.

I wonder if Patrick feels the same way, she thought. She had half expected that he'd be back by now, freshly shaved and showered and full of plans once more. Perhaps today they would go out to the beach for a swim, or just walk along the shore of Lake Michigan, or even stay home and just enjoy each other's company. . .

But he didn't turn up, and as time went on she began to feel edgy about it.

He's tired, she told herself. He must not have even

allowed himself to doze off last night, for fear of over-
sleeping. Maybe he just went home to bed, and after he's
rested——

Maybe he's not going to come back at all. The horrible
little thought, once it surfaced and demanded a hearing,
could not be pushed back into the far corner of her
brain. Maybe last night wasn't so special to him, the
demon at the back of her mind suggested. Maybe the
whole idea of taking you to meet his family was just
another seduction technique.

Stop it, she told herself. You're becoming paranoid.

She gave Susan a much-needed bath and an extra-
warm hug and settled her on a stool beside the centre
island to eat her breakfast. She listened half-heartedly to
the child's chatter about yesterday's party, punctuated
by bites of sausage and toast, and murmured an answer
now and then almost at random.

She was scrambling eggs to replenish the breakfast
buffet for her late-rising guests when a voice that seemed
to come out of nowhere said, 'Good morning, Camryn.'

She dropped her spoon; it rattled noisily against the
porcelain stove-top and then landed with a bang on the
floor. She turned; Susan was already down off her stool
and tugging at the kitchen door. Patrick was smiling at
her through the screened window beside it. He was his
neat, well-groomed everyday self again, complete with
tie and jacket, she saw, with a little tug of resentment.
So much for the idea of a peaceful afternoon's walk along
the beach. . .

'Susan!' she said sharply. 'You've got food all over
you. Go and wash your hands before you say hello to
Patrick.'

Susan looked up at her with astonishment in her wide

eyes at this unaccustomed tone of voice, and then went off slowly down the hall, her feet dragging.

'Sausage stains are greasy,' Camryn said abruptly, feeling guilty. 'It would be impossible to get them out of your jacket.' She bent to retrieve her spoon and put it in the sink. When she turned to get another, Patrick was right behind her.

'If that's a threat, I'll risk it,' he said, and cupped her face between his hands.

He explored her mouth in a long and leisurely kiss, with a hint of the previous night's wildness just beneath the surface. Camryn could feel her insides slowly becoming the consistency of hot fudge sauce.

He released her lips finally and smiled contentedly down at her as he pulled her even closer into his arms.

'Patrick,' she said. Her voice was unsteady. She wasn't quite sure what she intended to say, but what actually came out was, 'My scrambled eggs are going to burn.'

He let her go. 'How unromantic,' he mused, and leaned against the stove to watch as she finished stirring the concoction. After she dumped it, with an expert flip of the wrist, into a chafing-dish, he straightened up and said, 'Now can I kiss you?'

'After I take this to the dining-room.' But when she came back, she shook her head as he held out his arms. 'The toast-rack is empty, and the sausage is gone.' She stepped around him. 'Please, Patrick, you'll just have to stay out of the way.'

He stood there for a moment longer and looked thoughtfully down at her. Then he turned on his heel and went across the room to sit at the small table in the breakfast-room.

'Camryn,' he said, 'if you start the restaurant, it's always going to be like this.'

'It's not a restaurant, it's——'

'All right, call it what you want. It's still going to be this sort of rat race, all the time.'

She thought about it for a moment, while she turned sausages in the skillet.

Susan came back with clean hands. She ignored the remains of her breakfast and crept up on to Patrick's knee. The two of them had much the same look, Camryn thought, like a pair of thoroughly scolded puppies.

That is ridiculous, she thought. Then she smiled a little. Patrick had actually sounded jealous, she told herself. He didn't get the attention he wanted this morning—the attention he thought he deserved—so he's fussing about it. The idea gave her heart a lift.

'I'll be done in about an hour,' she said. 'The mess will be cleaned up, and the rest of the day is free.' It was a peace offering; would Patrick take it that way?

He glanced at the kitchen clock. 'That's time enough. I'll take you to brunch at the Lakemont Grand.'

So that was why he was dressed up! For an instant, her heart soared; she hadn't been to brunch at the newly renovated hotel downtown, because it was fearfully expensive. But she'd been longing to go. And now it was even more important, she admitted, because she was going with Patrick. . .

Then reality interfered. 'Sunday morning is a horrible time to find a baby-sitter,' she said, 'and Sherry's already gone for the day.'

Patrick looked a little disappointed. Susan's face clouded over and she slid off his lap and came across to her mother. She folded her arms and said mulishly, 'I don't want you to go out with Patrick.'

Camryn looked down at her in astonishment. This, she thought, is the last straw. If Susan is suddenly going to turn jealous, there isn't a chance in the world for this to work out. But how can the child possibly know that anything has changed? Yesterday, she certainly didn't mind. . .

'I don't think you need to worry about it,' she murmured. 'I'm not going.'

Patrick had followed the child. He dropped to one knee beside her and looked her straight in the eyes. 'Why don't you want her to go, Susan?'

She twisted her bare toes together and said, 'I want you to play with me instead, Patrick.'

His look up at Camryn was triumphant. 'I think we can solve this problem. Does the child own a dress?'

'A couple of them,' Camryn said drily. 'But you can't intend to take a four-year-old to brunch at a fancy hotel——'

'Why can't I? Is there a law against it?' He didn't wait for an answer. 'Take me up and show me your wardrobe, Susan, and we'll be waiting by the time your mother's done.'

The Lakemont Grand lived up to its name, and the big old ballroom, with its new face-lift, was the perfect spot for Sunday brunch. Camryn sipped her champagne and glanced at Susan, who was sitting quietly between them, eyes wide as she took in the scarlet and white room with its gilt trim and the huge murals on the ceilings. Good, Camryn thought. It looks as if I won't have to worry about her making a scene for a few minutes at least. She looks like a little angel.

She had kept her fingers crossed until Susan had danced into the kitchen to show off the dress they'd chosen; heaven only knew, she'd thought, what the pair of them might come up with! But the powder-pink dress with its matching hair-bow was probably the prettiest thing Susan owned. And Patrick must have ransacked the child's room to find a pair of lacy little stockings and her patent leather shoes—Susan loved to dress up, and Camryn had to keep that sort of thing hidden from her, or she would wear it out to play in the sandbox.

Thinking of sand reminded her of Dennis McKenna's front lawn. 'I must remember to write your parents a note about the incredible experience yesterday,' she said. 'I haven't even had a chance to tell you how much I enjoyed myself——'

'Oh?' He gave her a suggestive smile over the rim of his champagne glass. 'We might arrange a way, if you'd like to thank me.'

She had thought the day she had first met him that he had bedroom eyes, dark and sultry and surrounded with those absurdly long black lashes—eyes to make any woman envious. And it wasn't fair that he was looking at her that way in a public place. . .

Oh, at least be honest with yourself, she thought. He could look at you any way at all, and you'd melt, because it isn't the eyes at all, beautiful though they are. It's the man himself that you love, every charming and exasperating fragment of him.

He smiled at her as if he knew exactly what she was thinking, and before she could recover herself he took Susan out to dance. There were smiles all around the dance-floor at the dark-haired man and the tiny blonde girl, and an elderly woman stopped beside the table and said to Camryn, 'I just had to tell you what a beautiful little girl you have, and how lucky she is to have a father so devoted to her.'

Camryn's throat was tight. She managed to say 'Thank you,' and told herself there was no point in trying to explain. She was just grateful Patrick hadn't heard that one.

Perhaps, some day, it might be true, she thought, and then halted that line of thought with an effort, telling herself firmly to enjoy what she had and not to cry for what she didn't.

When the two of them came back, with Susan giggling at her first public treatment like a grown-up lady, Camryn concentrated on the mushroom omelette on her plate, and said firmly, 'About yesterday—I meant that your whole family is incredible.'

'Oh,' he murmured, 'you were talking about my family. I should have warned you, I know. It's sort of overwhelming for the uninitiated.'

'Overwhelming, yes. But very nice.'

'Thanks for taking Nell in, by the way. She'll enjoy having a vacation—and so will Mother.'

Camryn couldn't help laughing at the tone of his voice. 'Any two women who can share a house for years on end deserve a vacation now and then.'

'It's not so bad now. They really got into it once in a while, in the time before all of us kids left home.'

Camryn shivered. 'I couldn't imagine sharing my house with either of Susan's grandmothers. My mother never really liked Mitch, and——'

'Somebody actually didn't like Mitch the paragon?' He bit his lip. 'Sorry, Camryn.'

She decided that the only civilised thing to do was pretend that she hadn't heard him say it. 'And I was never very close to Mitch's mother. She seems to think material things are a substitute for personal contact. Take that dress Susan's wearing—she sent it last Christmas, but she didn't even bother to ask me what size Susan wore, and she's only now growing into it. You wouldn't believe the tears on Christmas morning when she couldn't wear her new dress.'

He reached across the table and put his hand on top of hers. His fingertips stroked the back of her wrist.

'Sorry,' she said. 'I didn't intend to be gloomy. I just meant to say that you're very lucky to have a family that cares.'

He didn't move, and he didn't speak.

The waiter put a crystal plate in front of her. On it was a picture-perfect crêpe, filled with ice-cream and topped with strawberries.

'The food's wonderful, isn't it?' she said, trying to recapture the mood. 'It's awfully nice to eat things I didn't make myself. . .'

Patrick drew back and picked up his fork. 'Camryn, we need to talk.' There was a note in his voice that reminded her unpleasantly of that first day in his office, before she had come to know what he really was like.

Suddenly, she was frightened of him. She moved Susan's glass of milk out of spilling range, cut up the child's crêpe, rearranged her napkin to cover the powder-pink dress. But she was only delaying. She knew it, and she also knew that Patrick wasn't fooled.

Finally, she had to look at him again.

'I want you to think very carefully about what I'm going to ask you to do,' he said. 'I've thought a lot about this, Camryn, and I'm not taking it lightly.'

Her heart started to pound, and she took a surreptitious grip on her napkin.

He looked down at his dessert plate as if gathering his courage, and then faced her. 'I don't want you to start the restaurant.'

For a long moment, the room spun crazily around her. Only the napkin that she was clutching seemed to be real, and then only because her fingers ached with the pressure she was exerting on it.

Not 'Will you, marry me?', as she had, she realised, been hoping. And not 'Will you share your life with me?', which she would find almost as appealing. In fact, it had not even been a question at all, when she stopped to think about it. It had really been an order!

'I see,' she said finally. There was a brittle quality in her voice.

It was obvious that he heard it. He leaned forward. 'Camryn, I don't think you understand the amount of labour you're taking on. You can't work twenty-four hours a day. You'll kill yourself trying to make a few extra dollars——'

'Don't you think that's my choice?'

'Is that what you want your life to be—just like this morning was? All that fuss and nonsense going on——'

'That fuss and nonsense is how I make my living, Patrick.'

'But every day? All day? And half the nights, as well? That's what it would take, Camryn.' He stared across at her for a long moment, and mused, 'And you're the one who didn't want to take a nine-to-five secretarial job.'

'I want to be at home with my daughter, yes.' She took a deep breath. 'I suppose all this is a prelude to suggesting again that I sell my house and leave her with a sitter——'

'That wasn't what I had in mind. But can you honestly say you'll be at home with her, when you'll be so busy you won't have time to notice what she's doing? She might as well be in day care.'

Camryn shot a look at Susan. So far, she didn't seem to be paying attention; she was dreamily surveying the crystal chandelier directly above her head. 'And what do you suggest I do? I have a solution; it seems incredibly irresponsible to me to sit around waiting to win the lottery instead!'

'Really, Camryn——'

'Do you have a better suggestion? You once said I should marry a wealthy man—perhaps you have a candidate in mind!'

His face was taut. 'Just don't be in such a rush——'

'Patrick, can we have this argument some other time, when Susan won't have to listen? Not that there is any point in continuing it; I am not going to give in. I am going to raise my daughter the way her father wanted——'

'Now that's a charming sentiment,' he drawled.

Camryn stared at him for a long moment. 'Just what do you mean by that?'

He set his coffee-cup down with a bang. 'I mean that it makes me furious to see you working and worrying like this and saying that you're doing it because it's what Mitch would have wanted. Damn Mitch! He obviously didn't care a rap about what happened to you and Susan——'

'That is enough!'

'It's not enough, not by a long way. Somebody has to open your eyes. It seems to me that when a man has a wife and a kid he ought to be concerned about them, more than about himself. Dammit, Camryn, your precious Mitch didn't even make an effort to provide for you——'

'Yes, he did!' she said in a furious undertone. 'He would have been a good provider. You forget that he didn't exactly die on purpose!'

'I know he didn't, but he seemed to think that being a doctor meant he had a guarantee on life. For a guy who was supposed to be so smart, he did some awfully dumb things——'

'I don't have to listen to this! I've given you no rights to tell me what to do!'

A muscle twitched at the corner of his mouth. 'What about last night, Camryn?' he said quietly.

'Last night didn't give you the right to talk to me like an army sergeant—the kind who thinks that bending the rules isn't good for people's moral development. Your set of rules includes me doing whatever you think is best—is that correct?'

He exhaled slowly, as if he was trying very hard to keep his temper. 'Don't over-react, Camryn. I didn't mean I wanted to take over your life. I just think you're getting tunnel-vision about this restaurant being the only answer to your problems. Don't close the door on your future——'

'The Stone House, and Susan, *are* my future. They're the only things I care about. And I will do whatever I have to do to survive.' She tossed her napkin down beside the crystal plate. 'Will you take us home, or shall I ask the doorman for a cab?'

For a long instant it seemed as if he hadn't even heard. He was looking at her, but he didn't seem to see her. His eyes were darker than she had ever seen them— dark, and hard, and distant.

He pushed his chair back, without a word.

Susan didn't want to leave her crêpe. Her face started to crumple at the idea, and Camryn thought, please, not this. So far today she's been a much better lady than I have—let's not ruin it with a scene as we go out of the door!

Patrick, too, seemed to have lost all patience. 'Put the damn thing in a box,' he told the waiter finally, and thrust it at Camryn when he caught up with her in the lobby after dealing with the bill. He didn't touch her, or Susan, again.

When they were half-way back to the Stone House, he said, as if the words were being forced out of him, 'Camryn, I'm sorry. I should have kept my mouth shut about Mitch.'

She bit her tongue hard, until she could say, without a quiver in her voice, 'If you hadn't meant it, I'm sure you wouldn't have said it. Don't regret it on my account, Patrick. I'm glad to know what you really think of me.'

'Dammit, that's not——'

'Your temper is getting the better of you again,' she pointed out.

He said something under his breath that she was glad Susan hadn't heard. She stared out of the window, and as the car drew up in front of the Stone House, he said quietly, 'Camryn, do what you think is best for yourself and Susan. But please—stop giving the credit to Mitch for what you've done yourself. Don't turn him into a hero.'

She gathered up the box that held Susan's crêpe, and reached into her handbag for her house key. Her fingers touched something soft. 'I keep forgetting to return this,' she said, and handed him a neatly ironed white square. And this, she thought, might be the last chance I ever have to give it to you. She forced the thought to the back corner of her mind. 'Your handkerchief—you were kind enough to lend it to me.'

'I thought you might keep it as a souvenir of another day, in another public place, when I made you cry.' He sounded disillusioned, and discouraged.

The memories of last night will be all the souvenirs I

need, she thought. He was watching her, she knew; she didn't look at him.

He sighed. 'I'll bring Nell over in the morning.'

Camryn stifled a groan. She had forgotten about Nell.

'And I'll take you to the bank as soon as it opens to talk to Warren about your plans.'

It should have made her happier that he was no longer going to fight her choice. But it didn't. 'I can get myself there, thank you.' Sheer perversity made her add, 'And the afternoon would be much better for me.'

'If you like,' he said finally. 'I was hoping to get it over with, myself.'

She stood inside the front door, the melting crêpe in her hand, and watched the car vanish around the corner.

I will not cry, she told herself. He isn't worth my tears.

CHAPTER NINE

ON MONDAY morning, Nell McKenna arrived, right on schedule. She appeared at the front door as if out of nowhere, carrying her own suitcase. A small, sporty red car was parked beside the garage, and Patrick—much to Camryn's relief—was not within sight. Nell did, however, have a tart comment about him not being gentleman enough to bring her over and carry her bag to her room, after which she very capably carried it upstairs herself and settled into the big front bedroom.

Thank heaven, Camryn thought, that Nell doesn't know the way he's been hanging around here drinking coffee and eating buns or she'd have enough questions to fuel the Spanish Inquisition!

Nell was back downstairs within fifteen minutes to announce that if Camryn had any plans to pamper her, she should forget them. 'My idea of a vacation is not to lie around on a chaise-longue and be waited on,' she said. 'I'd be miserable. In fact, I couldn't help noticing that you've got a few weeds in your garden. If you wouldn't mind, I'd like the exercise of hoeing them out. Don't worry about finding me a hat and gloves—I brought my own, just in case.'

Somehow, Camryn wouldn't have been surprised if she'd brought her own hoe, too. Before she could find her voice, Nell was outside attacking the weeds, with Susan and Ipswich along for company.

'She's certainly a fountain of energy,' Sherry said a couple of hours later, looking out of the window. 'We should all be so industrious at her age. She's even got Susan planting seeds.'

'And Ipswich is digging up the next row, I suppose.'

'No—he's chasing butterflies, and never catching them.'

'That's a relief.' Camryn didn't raise her head from the pile of papers spread on the breakfast-table. If she was going to make the best possible impression on Warren Stanford this afternoon, it was going to be up to her; she could obviously no longer rely on Patrick's whole-hearted backing. And if the man liked neat little columns of numbers, as Patrick had said he did, then she would do her best to make sure he had some to look at. If it took her all morning to reduce her plans to black and white, it would be worth it.

Sherry sat down across the table and glanced at the papers. 'Are you going to do weddings, too, Camryn? I mean, besides just receptions?'

'And throw in a honeymoon package, too? Why not?' Camryn didn't even look up. 'That's not a bad idea, Sherry—everything the bride and groom want for a warm homelike wedding, all in one location. I could ask for referrals from bridal shops and photographers, and——'

'That wasn't what I meant. I wasn't thinking of it as a business, exactly.'

'What were you thinking of?'

'Just that I'd like to be married here. I can picture myself floating down that gorgeous staircase in a cloud of lace, and saying my vows in front of the bay window in the living-room, with sunshine pouring over my dress. . .'

Camryn put her pencil down and looked speculatively across the table. 'Has John proposed yet?'

Sherry shook her head. 'No,' she said airily. 'But he'll get around to it.'

'I don't doubt he will, now that you've made up your mind.'

'He's got another year of residency.'

'He's also got a crazy mother.'

Sherry shrugged. 'If I can't get along with her, I'll just adopt a cat, and she'll keep her distance.'

'You're determined, I see.' Camryn turned back to her figures and added, 'Perhaps someone should warn the man that he's being stalked.' Her voice was tart, but there was relief in her soul that it wasn't settled yet. Finding a new renter for Sherry's apartment wouldn't present much of a problem, with the whole university community to draw from. But Sherry was far more than just a renter. Her willingness to help out with the work, her pleasant nature, her ability to be a friend to Camryn and to Susan as well—those things would not be easy to find again.

I hadn't even considered the possibility that she might leave, Camryn thought. How foolish of me not to remember that Sherry won't be in college forever.

Patrick had asked a lot of questions—what would happen if Camryn got sick, or if her clients stopped renting rooms. But nobody had considered what losing Sherry would mean.

And you haven't lost her yet, either, Camryn told herself. But you'd better remember this: when it comes right down to it, you've got only yourself to count on.

Sherry answered the telephone, and then handed it across to Camryn with concern raging in her face. 'It's the city health department,' she said. 'What are they after you for now?'

Camryn seized the telephone. 'Nothing. I called them

this morning with some questions about starting up my restaurant.' Now I'm doing it, too, she thought. It won't be a restaurant, but I'm going to have to find something better to call it.

Sherry went out to the terrace to study. In the garden, Susan had finished planting the world's crookedest row of green beans, and was lying on the grass looking for animal pictures in the clouds. Nell had shed her passionate-pink gardening gloves and had her fingers in the soil of the flower-bed that surrounded the birdbath. Ipswich had given up on butterflies and was stalking a bit of paper that had blown into the yard.

Camryn could see them all through the breakfast-room window. Everything was normal, everything was just as it should be. Except for the fact that on the other end of the telephone line the disembodied voice of a city health inspector was quietly blasting into smithereens the last, hard-fought hope Camryn had of salvaging her mortgage, her business—her life.

Nobody seemed to notice how quiet Camryn was for the rest of the day. Nell struck up a conversation about rosebushes with the woman next door, and before the afternoon was out she was invited over for coffee. Sherry went back to the campus for a class. Susan took her nap and then carried her box of coloured chalk outside and spent the rest of the afternoon turning the front path into a modern-art gallery, full of purple trees and psychedelic flowers and cats that looked like sticks held together with rubber bands.

Camryn went outside to admire the finished product and thought sadly that there wouldn't be many more afternoons like this. And then what, for them? An apartment somewhere?

I'll have to start looking for one, she thought. And for a job. How long would it take for the bank to foreclose and force them out of their house, anyway? Six months? A year?

I'll fight it every day that I can, she told herself, but the determination was short-lived. Fighting, too, would take cash—it cost money to hire lawyers, to pay court costs. And what would she gain, in the end? She would only delay the inevitable. Better to be realistic about it.

Besides, she told herself, do you really want to deal with Patrick for another year? Especially when it is an effort doomed to failure. . .

A failure. . .did she mean the house, or her love for Patrick himself? she wondered sadly. What had gone wrong? For a while she had been so certain that she loved him. . .

The trouble is, she told herself firmly, that you're still sure. You do love him. But he doesn't feel the same way. You convinced yourself that he cared, because you wanted so badly for him to love you. . .

For a moment, when his car pulled into the driveway, she thought that she had conjured him up out of sheer determination. Then the box of coloured chalks went flying on to the grass and Susan darted across the lawn, hands outstretched, calling his name.

I should stop her, Camryn thought. She's covered with chalk from head to toe, and a hug from her will turn him into a rainbow.

But she didn't. It will brush off, she told herself. And it serves him right.

He got out of the car and swung Susan up into his arms to carry her back across the lawn. He was headed straight for Camryn, and there was a stubborn expression on his face that she had seen before. It took all her strength of will to stand there and wait for him when what she really wanted to do was turn and run into the house.

This conversation has to be held some time, she thought. It might as well be now.

Patrick set Susan down. She was chattering about her pictures as she tugged him over to see what she had been doing, and Camryn cut across the flow of words. 'Susan, run into the house, please, and tell Nell that Patrick's here. She's in the solarium, I think.'

Patrick's jaw set, but he waited until Susan was out of hearing range before he said, 'I was only going to admire her chalk drawings. Is that on the forbidden list now, too?'

Camryn shrugged. 'I assumed that you wanted to see Nell.'

'As a matter of fact, I came to take her out to dinner.'

And for nothing else, his tone seemed to imply. He brushed a streak of chalk off the sleeve of his sports coat, as if it didn't really bother him but he needed something to do. 'You didn't come to the bank to keep your appointment today.'

She didn't answer.

'Why, Camryn?' The hardness had gone out of his voice. 'Are you having second thoughts about the restaurant, after all? Are you thinking of giving it up?'

She said coldly, 'Now that I've had a chance to consider your persuasive remarks and realise that of course you must be right—is that what you mean?'

His face seemed to freeze. 'That catty attitude doesn't suit you very well.'

'I'm sorry to have to disappoint you, Patrick, but your plans for the improvement of my personality are really of no interest to me.' She turned towards the house. She was trembling inside, shocked by her own hatefulness, and somehow unable to get herself switched back to a more pleasant track. I'm going to have to tell him what happened today, she thought, and why I didn't come to the bank. I owe him an explanation. And why make the explanation harder on me by putting it off, and being snappy about it.

He followed her, of course. She led the way up to the solarium as if he'd never been there before. Nell looked up from the patch she was applying to the worn-out knee of a pair of Susan's jeans. Camryn wondered briefly where the woman had found them.

'Hello, Patrick. So you decided to check up on me.'

He smiled at his grandmother as charmingly as if everything was perfectly normal. 'I thought you might be getting hungry by now. This isn't a bed-and-three-meals-a-day, after all, just breakfast. I forgot that when we made the arrangements.'

And he's laying the groundwork for moving her out of here, too, Camryn thought. He doesn't want to come back, where he might have to see me. The logic nearly froze her heart. What happened to us, Patrick? she wanted to scream. We had so much to share. . .

'Oh, Camryn and I settled that this morning,' Nell said comfortably. 'She's making an exception for me. Tonight it's roast beef.'

'Since I'm cooking for Susan and Sherry and me anyway, it's no extra bother,' Camryn said stiffly.

'So you don't need to worry about me, Patrick,' Nell went on. She shook out the jeans and started on the other knee. 'In fact, if you're very nice, Camryn might be persuaded to stretch dinner to feed one more.' She bit off a thread. Her blue eyes held the barest trace of malicious mischief, but her voice was innocent. 'It seems only fair. We're putting it on your bill, of course.'

Patrick shook his head.

He didn't even have to think about it, Camryn told herself. He can't wait to get out of here. . .

'I'd better check on dinner,' she said, and beat a hasty retreat to her kitchen.

What did you expect? she asked herself angrily as she bent over the roasting pan in the oven. The minute he got out of his car you began treating the man like an infectious disease—of course he doesn't want to stick around for more of that!

And I don't want him to stay, either, she lectured firmly. Not after the things he said to me yesterday, and the way he seemed to think that I should kneel down and kiss his hand in gratitude!

But that was still no excuse for the way she was behaving, she admitted. After all, he had tried to find a solution to her problems. And even yesterday, with the whole discussion of the restaurant—well, they disagreed on lots of things, but she had to admit that he'd been perfectly sincere. Surely he deserved a little credit for that? It wasn't his fault that nothing was working out right.

'Camryn.' It was soft, almost a whisper.

She didn't even turn around. She pushed the roasting pan back into the oven and put her oven gloves carefully away in the drawer. 'I'm sorry for being catty to you, Patrick.'

He moved so quietly that it startled her when he spoke from directly behind her. 'Why didn't you come to the bank this afternoon?'

'Because it wouldn't have done any good.'

'Don't you think Warren should decide that?'

'He would have turned me down.' She took a bag of carrots out of the refrigerator and started to pare them. 'You got your wish, Patrick—I won't be starting my luncheon and tea business. There are just too many regulations.' She steadied her voice with an effort. 'I talked to the people in the city health department today, and they explained that the bed and breakfast rules were specially written to encourage people to start small— they have to be, or no one could afford to go into the business. But serving food to people who aren't staying here would make me a restaurant.' Just saying it made it worse; the pain was threatening to drown out her voice. 'Please, don't say I told you so——'

'I wasn't going to.'

'To do it, I'd have to comply with all of the city's rules for commercial kitchens. About twenty thousand dollars' worth of improvements and I might be able to open,' she added bitterly.

'I'm sorry, Camryn.'

'No, you're not.'

He hadn't sounded surprised. She thought about that, and fleetingly wondered why. He tried to talk me out of it, she thought, and when that didn't work, did he arrange for this to happen? No, she told herself. You really can't get by with putting the blame for this on Patrick.

He certainly hadn't been behind that call from the inspector this morning; she'd been the one who had called to ask the health department for the rules. Even if he had wanted to interfere, the regulations couldn't have been manufactured this morning just to suit Patrick McKenna's wishes. There were volumes of them. . .

Perhaps he knew about the rules, she thought, and he

knew what a blow it would be to me. Perhaps he was trying to keep me from being hurt. . .

But if that was the case, she thought severely, he could have tried telling the truth.

She finished the carrots and looked up at him with a challenge in her eyes. 'So that's why I didn't come to see Warren Stanford today—I didn't have anything new to tell him. I'm right back at the beginning, again, and I'm running out of time.'

'I'm sorry, Camryn——'

'Would you stop saying you're sorry? I don't need your pity.' It came out more sharply than she had intended, and she said, a little more gently, 'I thought perhaps you had something in mind yesterday, before we got into the argument about the restaurant—some alternative, so I can keep my house.'

For an infinite moment, the only sound in the room was the soft purr of the exhaust fan above the stove. 'Not an alternative, exactly,' he mused. 'I was going to ask you to marry me.'

The exhaust fan seemed suddenly as loud as the roaring of a freight train. Camryn's hands clenched on the edge of the stainless-steel sink; without its support, she would have slid to the floor. My dearest dream, she thought, for one infinitesimal instant.

And then she realised that he had said, 'Not an alternative, exactly.' Just what did that mean? That his proposal was based on conditions? Her refusal to give up the idea of the restaurant yesterday had obviously been very important to him; if he had really loved her, and honestly wanted to marry her, wouldn't he have said so anyway?

'But you just didn't get around to it, is that it?' Her voice was light. 'Because I didn't co-operate? Have I got it straight—you were going to bail me out, but only if I gave up the restaurant? How charming of you, Patrick. Tell me, are there any other terms I should know about?'

His face had hardened, and a tiny muscle twitched at the corner of his mouth.

'Is it enough that there won't be a restaurant, or are there a few other things about my life you'd like to change? You've said often enough that I should just get rid of the Stone House altogether—is that part of the price for having you?'

'I don't exactly see a bed and breakfast in my life forever, no.' It was calm. 'There are other ways, Camryn——'

'Aren't you being a little hypocritical? You implied yesterday that Mitch was a criminal fool for wanting me to be a wife and not have a profession——'

Sherry pushed open the swinging door between the kitchen and the dining-room and came half-way in. 'When will——?'

'Not now, Sherry!' Camryn almost screamed at her. She flung her head back and looked defiantly up at Patrick. 'I don't see much difference, you know. Mitch didn't want me to have a job—now you want me to give up the one I have and find something else, one that pleases you better. Is this a new application of the golden rule, perhaps—"He who hath the most gold maketh the rules"? Is that your idea of how marriage ought to work, Patrick? What a disappointment for you!'

Sherry spun on her heel with military precision and vanished down the hall.

Patrick leaned against the centre island. 'You don't even realise how angry you are at him, do you, Camryn?' He sounded perfectly calm, almost clinically detached. 'He deserted you, and you're determined not to let yourself be put in that position again, of depending on a man——'

'He didn't desert me.'

'It doesn't matter whether he did it on purpose or not; the fact is he left you in the lurch. But you don't even see that, do you, Camryn? You haven't even faced up to that——'

'At least Mitch was honest about what he wanted; he didn't go around manipulating me! I am damned sure going to make my own decisions, Patrick—that's not in question! I appreciate your flattering proposal. But no, thanks——'

He pushed himself away from the island. 'Haven't you forgotten something? I didn't actually propose to you. I only said I'd been planning to—once.'

'I was going to ask you to marry me.' Past tense, with no hint of a future. . .

'Actually,' he said, 'I'm beginning to think it was a damned lucky escape. Thanks, Camryn—you've certainly put things in perspective.'

It hurt so badly that for an instant she was terrified she was going to faint. But then she straightened her spine and put her head up and said, 'I'm in good company, aren't I? Right up there with Dianna Stanford, among the girls you've considered proposing to. I'm so flattered I can hardly stand it.'

For a moment she thought he wasn't going to answer. Then he said quietly, 'You should be. You finished better than I did—I lost out to Mitch's ghost. It's just as well, I suppose. The Stone House isn't big enough for the three of us, Camryn—you and me and Mitch.'

The outside door slammed behind him, as if he couldn't wait any longer to get out into the open air. In the long moment when the sound still echoed through the kitchen, Camryn sank down on a stool and buried her face in her hands.

You've messed it all up now, she told herself. You've lost them both—the Stone House, and Patrick as well. . .

No, I didn't, she thought. It wasn't all my doing. It was Patrick's.

But the question of which of them had been most at fault didn't matter right now. She just wanted to throw herself down across her bed and cry. She didn't even know for which one—the Stone House, or Patrick—she would shed the most tears.

Sherry took one swift glance at the dining-room table, set for four, and said, 'Patrick's not staying?'

'Did you expect him to?' Camryn retorted.

'Well, no, I guess not. From the bit I heard, that must have been a king-sized fight you two were having.'

Camryn scowled at her. Didn't the girl even have enough sense to be quiet in front of a guest—especially this guest?

Sherry finally seemed to get the message. 'Sorry,' she muttered, with a sidelong glance at Nell.

Camryn suppressed a shudder, with great effort. Nell was capable of asking anything at all. If Nell starts on me, she thought, I will just start to scream and throw knives.

But Nell didn't seem to notice anything unusual in the air. She tucked a napkin under Susan's chin and sat down beside her, inhaling with gusto. 'That beef smells magnificent, Camryn,' she said. 'Do you have some magical way of cooking it?'

She talked gently all the way through dinner, and finally Camryn's knotted nerves began to relax.

Life hasn't come to an end, she told herself. And I've survived worse, and come out of it stronger than before. I still have Susan, and my health. Perhaps I can find some sort of job that will allow me to finish my education. And some day there can be another house. . .

And another Patrick, too, I suppose, she told herself cynically. Now that I've found out that I still have physical longings, I should probably start looking for a man to satisfy them with!

Her heart twisted at the very thought of that faceless someone—a man who wasn't Patrick. A man who could never, never be Patrick. . .

The evening had a sort of a sort of breathless stillness to it. The solarium windows were all open, and the ceiling fan lazily stirred the warm air. Camryn was curled up in the window-seat in the corner of the room, looking listlessly out over the street and remembering how Sherry had sat there last weekend in the same pose, waiting hopelessly for John Marlow to call.

But Sherry had been the lucky one. John had called. And Camryn had no doubt that, unless Sherry changed her mind, in one more year she would marry John Marlow, and they'd live happily ever after. But the wedding wouldn't take place at the Stone House.

She drew idle patterns on the screen with her fingernail and watched the birds play in the birdbath in the back yard. And she didn't know that she had made a sound until Nell said, 'That sigh sounded as if your heart was breaking, Camryn. Would it help to talk about it?'

Talk about it? she thought helplessly. Tell Patrick's own grandmother what a chauvinistic, domineering brute he was? Or, worse yet, confide in Nell the fact that she loved him anyway?

'I don't think so,' she said drearily.

Nell didn't answer. She had laid aside the patched jeans; she had, it appeared to Camryn, worked her way through the entire contents of the Stone House's mending-basket in one short afternoon. Somewhere she had found a scrap of tightly woven cotton fabric and some bits of brightly coloured thread, and now she was patiently instructing Susan in some elementary embroidery techniques. The child lacked co-ordination, and her stitches were uncertain and wildly inaccurate, but she seemed to be having a good time. Her tongue was protruding a bit, as it often did when she was really concentrating, and her forehead wrinkled now and then.

'How have you managed to raise such a feminine child?' Nell asked. 'Of course, I'm sure it's easier when there's only one. I tried, with Dennis and Kathleen's youngest—but with four older brothers, the girl was too much a tomboy to save.'

That's a funny thing for Nell to say, Camryn thought idly. I'd have said that she's got a fair amount of tomboy blood herself, with the horseshoes and all.

But Nell looked a little more like a standard grandmother today, wearing a softly printed blouse and comfortable trousers, and sitting in the rocking-chair with Susan in her lap and the mending-basket beside her, with a pair of half-glasses balanced on her nose. Only the name-brand running shoes hinted that she might not really be what she appeared.

'It's difficult to raise children alone,' Nell said.

Camryn braced herself. What is coming next? she wondered. A gentle lecture on why I should marry Patrick? If Nell only knew how clear he made it that I haven't been asked!

Susan stabbed her finger with the needle, and she

howled and looked up at Nell for comfort. Nell kissed the small wounded finger, smoothed the fabric with a work-worn hand, applauded the effort, and put it away for the night.

I wish I was the one sitting beside Nell, Camryn thought, in the circle of a reassuring arm, and being helped and comforted. . .I don't have to tell her about Patrick, after all. I would make me feel better just to be able to tell someone about the damned mortgage. . .

She never quite knew how she ended up across the room, with her head in Nell's lap, sobbing out the whole story, complete with every instant of hope and every traumatic blow. And all the time, Nell didn't say a word, just sat very still, her fingers stroking Camryn's hair now and then as if she were no older than Susan. . .

Finally, she sighed. 'You haven't tried any other banks?'

If the question had come from anyone else, Camryn thought hazily, I'd probably feel offended. But from Nell. . .'No,' she said. 'It does sound dumb, doesn't it? But Patrick was helping me, and I thought surely I stood a better chance there, where they knew me, where I already had a record of always paying my bills on time.' She smiled wryly. 'Well, almost always on time.'

'What does Patrick think?'

'He says——' Camryn stopped, and corrected herself. 'He said once that if it were up to him, he would give me the loan. But his boss——'

Nell snorted. 'That figures. I never could abide that stuffed shirt Patrick works for. Warren Stanford shouldn't be a banker—he ought to own a used-car garage in California. He's an expert at buying money at one end of the building and selling it back to the same people at the other end at a higher price.'

'But surely that's a banker's business——?'

'Yes, it is. What I can't stand is the way he tries to imply that you're getting a bargain!'

Camryn laughed. She blew her nose and settled herself more comfortably on the rug at Nell's feet with her knees drawn up and her arms clasped around them. 'I don't like him, either. But I could be polite to anyone who'd give me that loan, and he's in the business of lending money.'

'Doesn't sound much like it,' Nell grumbled.

'And now Patrick——' Camryn swallowed hard. 'Well, he's very angry with me just now, so I'm afraid I can't count on him for help any more.'

'Patrick is a lot of things, including hot-headed and foolish and judgemental, but he isn't petty. And he is a businessman. He isn't going to deny you a loan just out of the sheer, perverse pleasure of seeing you driven out of your home.'

'Well, I'm not counting on him helping any more.' Camryn muttered. 'I think it would make Patrick very happy indeed if I had to give up the Stone House.'

Nell didn't answer. Her lips were pursed thoughtfully.

What an idiot you are, Camryn told herself, to forget who you're talking to. She pasted a smile on her face and looked up at Nell, intending to carry it off as a sort of joke. But the old woman's brightly inquisitive eyes seemed to reach into her soul.

Camryn's voice was unsteady. 'In any case, it isn't going to matter what Patrick thinks, in the long run. They're going to foreclose.'

'Unless you can find a way to convince Warren Stanford that you're good for the money,' Nell said comfortably. She started to rock again; the chair had a rhythmic squeak that was almost soothing.

As if it was no problem, Camryn thought. But she shouldn't blame Nell for thinking it was not an insurmountable obstacle; she herself had thought the same thing at first.

'Or unless someone else will vouch for you. Is that right?'

'Right,' Camryn said drearily. 'But it isn't all that easy, Nell. Not just anyone off the street is going to guarantee my loan—after all, it means they may end up paying it, if I don't. The damnable thing about it is that I know I can do it, because I have been doing it.' She struck her fist against a cushion. 'But nobody else seems to believe me. At least not enough to back me up.'

Nell rocked gently for half a minute. Then she said softly, 'I do, Camryn. And I'll guarantee your loan.'

CHAPTER TEN

CAMRYN'S first reaction was amusement; Nell McKenna obviously did not understand that Warren Stanford would not accept just anyone's word when it came to guaranteeing a mortgage loan.

He will probably listen to her very patiently as she tells him just what a nice, reliable person I am, Camryn thought, and then usher her out of the door and laugh behind her back. . .

'Nell, I doubt Mr Stanford will think your guarantee is adequate,' she said, doing her best to be gentle about it.

'Oh, he may not take my word for it,' Nell said placidly. 'He doesn't have a very high opinion of women—or hadn't you noticed? But if I back up my promise with a large deposit in his silly bank—a deposit the same size as your mortgage, for instance. . .' The rocking-chair squeaked gently, rhythmically.

Camryn discovered that her mouth was hanging open. She shut it with difficulty and said weakly, 'Do you mean you could actually do that?'

'I've made a little money from my hobby over the years.'

'That's not "*a little money*", Nell—it's a fortune. And just what kind of hobby?'

After a long moment, Nell said, 'I've played around in the stock market.' It was the same tone of voice as if she had been admitting to a secret fondness for pornographic movies.

Camryn swallowed hard. 'Nell, I never dreamed that you——'

'I'm sure you didn't, dear.'

Nell's tone was perfectly flat and calm, and suddenly cold fear washed over Camryn. Had there been a note of sarcasm in that matter-of-fact voice? Did Nell think this was all some sort of con game? Did she believe that Camryn had known about her money all along, and that she had cold-bloodedly planned how to win the old woman's sympathy? And was she going along with it anyway, for reasons of her own?

Camryn cleared her throat and said harshly, 'If I had even suspected, I'd never have told you about my mortgage.'

'That would have been a pity, don't you think? Do be reasonable, child. I haven't lived this many years without being able to recognise a scheme when I see one, and I know that you're quite incapable of organising such a thing.' She rocked tranquilly for a moment, and added, before Camryn could make up her mind whether or not to be insulted, 'Patrick could. But I've made it a point never to discuss money with him. I didn't want him to start nagging me about putting mine in a safer place—such as his bank.'

'But if you dislike that bank, why would you even consider putting all that money in it?'

'Oh, it doesn't matter so much now. I don't trust banks as a general rule—they tend to be more interested in the stockholder's profits than in the depositors'. But then I'm not so concerned about the return on my investment as I used to be. Heaven knows I don't need to worry any more about providing for my declining years—I'm already in them.'

Decline, Camryn thought. If she's in a decline, then

I'd hate to have been around when she was active; it woud have been impossible to keep up with her. She shook her head in astonishment. 'I still don't understand. All the fuss about who was going to pay for your week here—I was right there, Nell, and I heard the argument——'

'There's no need to spend my money if Patrick is willing to spend his,' Nell pointed out cheerfully.

'Not that I'm going to charge for your stay,' Camryn added hastily. 'I wouldn't think of it. But——'

'What kind of businesswoman are you, Camryn? You'd better charge, or I'll think twice about risking my money with you.' Nell added, with a sly grin, 'Besides, it's Patrick's bill—remember? Not mine. Right up until you marry him, I'll be a guest of the paying variety. After that. . .'

The floor seemed to rock a little under Camryn's feet. Of course, she thought. That's why she's willing to bail me out. She thinks she's helping Patrick as well.

She closed her eyes for a moment against the pain that had suddenly started to throb in her head, so strong that it was threatening to take the top of her skull off. There was only one thing to do, she told herself. She could not take advantage of Nell like that; she had to tell her the truth, even if that put an end to this new hope.

'I'm not going to marry him,' she said quietly.

Nell raised her eyebrows. 'Oh? May I ask why not?'

Camryn wanted to swear. What am I supposed to say? she wondered, and decided that the less she told Nell, the better. 'Mainly because I wasn't asked. That wasn't just a lovers' quarrel tonight, Nell. It was—final.' She swallowed hard. 'If that makes a difference about the mortgage, I understand, of course. I should have told you before.'

Nell looked astounded. 'Should it make a difference?'

'Doesn't it?'

'Of course not. I'm not concerned about having to make good on my promise, with or without Patrick. But in any case, I wouldn't give up on him just yet, Camryn. And remember, my dear, that one has to make allowances. A young man in love isn't exactly the most rational creature on earth.'

Camryn didn't pursue the discussion. *Don't give up on him*, she thought wryly. As if I would still want him!

But surely it wasn't necessary for her to destroy Nell's illusions; time would do that soon enough. She had told the woman the truth, after all. If Nell wanted to convince herself that black was white, that certainly wasn't Camryn's problem.

That night, in the middle of her bedtime ritual, Susan asked why Patrick hadn't stayed to play with her.

Camryn could have kicked herself for not foreseeing the question and having an answer prepared. 'He was busy tonight, honey. He really just came to see Nell, anyway.'

'Sherry told Nell you were fighting with him,' Susan observed. 'Were you?'

Sherry should be taken out and shot, Camryn thought grimly. She tried to keep her voice calm. 'We had a disagreement, yes. Does Freddy Bear want a kiss tonight?'

Susan held him up. 'When is he coming to see us again?'

You cannot lie to her, Camryn told herself. And yet— *never* sounded so needlessly cruel. 'I don't know, dear,' she said softly, 'Off to sleep now.'

Susan snuggled obediently down into her soft blankets, and Camryn went downstairs to sit at her desk in the breakfast-room, where not even Sherry would dare disturb her.

She'll forget, she told herself. Given a little time, Susan will forget all about this charming man named Patrick.

But will you forget, Camryn? she asked herself. Will you some day be reminded of him, and say with a smile, 'Oh, yes, once upon a time I was in love with Patrick McKenna. . .'

She tried to remind herself of the fury she had felt tonight. But she could only remember how much it had hurt when he said he had had a lucky escape.

That should answer the question, she told herself. He couldn't really love me—not with the things he said to me.

You said some things to him, too, the little voice of conscience reminded—things that weren't approved by any etiquette book. You shouldn't hold him to a higher standard than you use for yourself.

A young man in love isn't exactly the most rational creature on earth. . .

Well, Camryn thought, she certainly agreed with Nell on certain portions of that statement—he wasn't rational, that was for sure. He had asked her to do things that no woman in her right mind would do for any man. Give up her home——

But had he asked that, really? the little voice in the back of her brain asked. Or had she been jumping to conclusions? He had certainly spent the better part of his days lately trying to get her money so she could keep the house——

Or had he just made it look as if he was trying?

She shook her head in frustrated confusion. She had been so angry, and now she could not remember.

It doesn't matter what he said about the house, anyway, she told herself. What he said about Mitch is unforgivable enough, all by itself. How dare he imply that Mitch was a reckless fool who only cared about himself? What gives him the right to say that Mitch didn't really give a damn about me or about Susan?

Stop it, Camryn, she told herself. You're gaining nothing by going over and over this. You've already concluded that you had a lucky escape, too, when Patrick decided against proposing to you. Why drag it all out for an inquest? He doesn't matter. He certainly doesn't care about the things that are important to you. . .

Things like Susan? the querulous little voice in the back of her brain demanded. Are you saying that he doesn't care about Susan? He's spent more time with her in a week than Mitch did in the entire six months he had a daughter. . .

She closed her eyes, and bits of memory attacked her from all sides: Patrick, carrying Susan up to bed; Patrick, teaching her to dance; Patrick, not minding chocolate and grime and chalk smeared all over him in enthusiastic greeting. . .

'Mitch would have had a fit,' she said under her breath. 'And he would have blamed me, because it was my job to keep her clean.'

It was like a dam breaking in her mind—the first tiny chink appearing, harmless-looking, releasing only a trickle of memory. But then the trickle became a flood. . .

Mitch had never changed a nappy in his life. 'He was busy,' Camryn defended, automatically. But she could remember him pointedly handing Susan over to her to be changed. And he had hated it when she cried. . .

'She was only a baby when he died,' she muttered. 'It would have changed as she developed more personality. Mitch loved kids—he wanted lots of them——'

Perfect kids, she thought. Ones that were always surgically clean and cute and smiling. Kids who would grow up to be quarter-backs and valedictorians and heart surgeons and campus beauty queens.

She pushed her chair back amost violently, as if by leaving the breakfast-room she could break the pattern of her thoughts. But she found herself a few minutes later in the living-room, in front of the big colour portrait taken on their wedding day, as if she had been drawn there by a rope.

She stared at the pair of people in the portrait. Mitch, already the assured young doctor. Camryn, the sweet and pliable little wife. Both of them strangers to her, now.

For the first time, she forced herself to think about what would have happened if Mitch had lived. What would her life be like? What would tonight—the average Monday evening in July—have held?

What she saw brought a chill to her heart. There would not be money problems in the Stone House, she was certain of that. There would not be paying guests upstairs in the main bedrooms. There might, or might not, be another child in the nursery—that would depend, she thought, on how Mitch had really felt about Susan, and she was no longer quite sure of that.

But nothing much else would be different. The house would be quiet, with Susan in bed. Mitch would almost certainly not be home; if he wasn't at the hospital, he would be at the gym, or playing cards with his buddies— or in Canada, hunting or fishing.

And what about me? she asked dispassionately. Would

I be happy here tonight, waiting for Mitch? Or would I be just one more bored housewife, looking for an alternative in food or alcohol—or any man who was handy? Could I have fitted forever into the mould that looked so inviting when I was nineteen years old and in love?

But Mitch had died, and of necessity Camryn had grown up.

'Don't turn him into a hero,' Patrick had said. 'Stop giving the credit to Mitch for what you've done yourself.'

I've been alone for over three years, she thought, and I've changed—I've grown. Losing Mitch made me stronger and more complete than I could ever have been as his wife.

Mitch would have hated me to be like this, she thought. He wanted me to be Mrs Mitchell Hastings— he needed that, somehow, to prove he was worthwhile. He wanted that image, of a wife at home, waiting for him, depending on him——

And I would have hated him for it, after a while, she thought. Instead, Mitch had died, and she had learned to stand on her own.

And now she felt lucky—not grateful that he had died; she could never feel anything like that, for she had loved him. But she felt lucky to have escaped from the trap she had built so contentedly, so easily, with her own hands. . .

It was a paradox, she concluded. Now that she didn't need a man to give her support, dignity, identity, she had more to offer than she had ever had before. Because she didn't have to depend on a man, she would be better able to share her life with him. . .

'The problem with that,' she told herself, 'is that the man I want doesn't want me.'

And she did still want Patrick, she conceded, finally.

The real question was whether she had waited too late to admit that he had seen her more clearly than she could see herself.

After all of the fuss, the worry, the plans and the work, it seemed hardly possible that a mortgage could be so easy to get after all. Her application was approved within minutes after she and Nell sat down in Warren Stanford's office the following afternoon. He was all that was charming and gracious as he renewed his acquaintance with Nell and made polite conversation about everything that had happened to both of them in the intervening years. It was apparent to Camryn that Nell was having trouble keeping her temper over what she obviously considered to be nosy questions, but on the whole she restrained her inclination to sarcasm and applied charm by the quart instead. Camryn thought it would have been funny to watch Nell playing the clinging vine, if only the whole matter hadn't been so important.

And, she admitted reluctantly, if only Patrick had been there to share the joke. But he wasn't anywhere to be seen.

When they had first entered the bank, the sight of his darkened office had come as a relief to Camryn. She needed to make her apologies, and that couldn't be done here, in front of Nell and Warren Stanford.

Besides, she thought, it would be difficult enough when he found out what his grandmother was doing, and Camryn didn't have the strength of mind to sit quietly and listen to the explanations and discussions. He might be angry, or annoyed, or piqued that he hadn't known Nell had that sort of resources.

Or what would be even harder to bear, Camryn admitted to herself, was that he might shrug it off with relief that he didn't have to be bothered with her financial problems any more.

As the interview went on, however, and no mention was made of Patrick, she began to get nervous. Just where was he, on a Tuesday afternoon?

Out with a client, she told herself. That's all. Remember that he has more people to worry about than just you, Camryn.

Warren Stanford shuffled papers and pushed some across the desk for Camryn to sign. 'Patrick will be very happy to know this is all settled,' he said. 'Too bad he's taking the afternoon off; he'd have liked to be in at the finish, I know.'

'I'll have to talk with him about skipping work,' Nell muttered. 'Now that I'm putting some money in this organisation, I'll expect him to stick around and keep an eye on it.'

Warren Stanford laughed. It was a social, meaningless sound. 'That's a good one. I'll tell him. As a member of fact, he's having tea with my Dianna this afternoon, at home.'

Camryn's hand clenched so tightly on her pen that she was surprised it didn't crack in her grip. That didn't take him long, she thought. Last night he was thinking of proposing to me. Today he's having tea with Dianna. . .

She had a sudden vision of an endless row of tea-tables, each groaning under the weight of hundreds of rich pastries and elegant desserts. Tea with Dianna—if it was anything like her picnic had been, it would certainly be an occasion!

Well, she told herself flatly, if that's what he wants, then I'm glad he's found it out now. If he had proposed to me, or married me, and then discovered that Dianna was what he wanted after all. . .

That would truly have broken my heart, she admitted quietly. To have been promised happiness, and actually to have held it in my hand like a bright-coloured helium balloon, and then to have it snatched away by a freak, uncaring breeze——

'Dianna thinks he's a very special young man, Nell,' Warren Stanford went on. 'And so do I. They've had their quarrels, you know, but I'm confident they'll get it all straightened out in the end.' He smiled and pushed his chair back. 'Now I'll just take all this paperwork out to the teller's window, and we'll be in business.'

The door closed behind him with a well-bred little whoosh, and Nell snorted. 'That man was always a snake!'

Camryn clasped her hands together against the soft fabric of her bronze-coloured skirt. It kept them from shaking quite so much. 'He has good reason to think that Patrick and Dianna——' She stopped. It hurt too much to couple their names like that. 'It would help his career.'

'Don't you be wishy-washy,' Nell ordered. 'Just because Warren Stanford thinks it's important, it doesn't mean it is. I wouldn't worry—tea with Dianna, indeed! Patrick has better sense than to think career advancement is worth that.'

Camryn didn't argue. There would have been no point to it, and there was no opportunity; Warren Stanford was soon back, and then the interview was all over. He crushed Camryn's hand in his big one, his diamond pinky ring cutting into her fingers. She bore the pain without comment; it helped to erase the vacant numbness in her heart. And she tried to feel truly happy that her house was safe.

Surely she should feel glad about that? she told herself. After all, that was the important thing—the only really important thing that was left

She sent Patrick a note the next day, thanking him for all the time and effort he had put forth. That was all. The rest of what she had to say couldn't be put down on paper. It would have to wait until she saw him.

But when days went by and he didn't come—didn't even stop to see Nell—she knew that it was truly over. So she went back to living as they had before, taking Susan to the park, developing new varieties of applesauce muffins, welcoming her guests and taking care of them, trying—without much success—to keep herself too busy to think.

When Kathleen McKenna called to announce that the painters were gone and the house was completely aired out, Camryn was sincerely sorry. She had grown attached to Nell in one short week, and the Stone House seemed to echo after the old woman was gone. She listened to the sounds it made for a couple of hours and then, unable to stand any more, took Susan to the library to spend the afternoon.

When they came out, they sky had darkened, and a summer thunderstorm was threatening. 'So much for my good idea of a walk,' she muttered. 'We may get wet, Susan.'

But she had underestimated the storm; before they had gone a block, the first huge drops of rain were splattering on the path. She hesitated for an instant in front of the Lakemont National Bank. Don't be a fool, she thought. You're going to be drenched through if you don't get inside. Besides, you have to come back here some day—you've got money in your handbag that should be deposited. Why not take care of it today? Then Patrick—then no one can question why you're here.

She pulled Susan inside and fumbled in her bag for the week's cheques. The teller made the requisite comments about the weather and smiled as she handed back the receipt and a lollipop for Susan. Camryn thanked her and turned towards the door. 'We'll wait out in the entrace till the storm's over, Susan——' she began, before she realised that Susan wasn't beside her any more.

And of course there was only one place the child would have gone. Camryn turned towards the executive wing. There might still be time to catch her. . .

She arrived in the doorway of Patrick's office just in time to see Susan climbing up on his knee to give him a hug. At least she's clean, for a change, Camryn thought. Wet, but clean. . .

And obviously confident of her welcome, she added to herself. I wish I were as certain of what would happen if I were to walk over there and put my arms around him. . .

The pain caused by the mere thought made her voice a little stiff. 'I'll take her out of your way,' she said. 'Susan doesn't understand business, I'm afraid.'

Patrick turned his chair around from the window. 'She's not interrupting anything. Or are you anxious to get her away from my bad influence?'

'Of course not.'

'Then it's for yourself that you're avoiding me?'

It was like a slap of cold water in her face. 'From my point of view, it looks as if you're the one doing the avoiding. You didn't even stop to see your grand-mother——'

'You expected me to?'

Camryn's gaze dropped to the carpet as she remembered that last quarrel. 'No, I suppose I didn't. Patrick——'

'Besides, it sounds as if she didn't miss me in the least. Nell gave me quite a glowing review of her stay—that's a bit unusual, for her. Of course, since she has decided to back the place——'

'So that's what's making you irritable. I assure you, Patrick, I didn't ask her for the help.' The silence drew out into a fragile eon of time, and Camryn thought, what's the use of trying to explain, to apologise? 'Come along, Susan.'

Susan didn't move from her comfortable perch. 'It's still raining,' she said wisely. 'We'll get wet.' She reached for the gold pen from Patrick's desk set and started to write her name on his blotter.

'You're walking?'

She glanced ruefully at the dark sky outside the window. 'Well, it didn't look like rain when we left.'

'I'll take you home.' He set Susan off his lap and stood up. 'Don't argue, Camryn—it isn't going to let up any time soon, and I was going to come by anyway and pay Nell's bill. That's what she called me about—to tell me that she wasn't letting me off the hook for her expenses.'

'There's no bill.'

'Is that any way to run a business?'

'That's exactly what she said. Nevertheless, I think I owe you both something—you for all your efforts——'

'I know how appreciative you are. I got your note.' It was cool, ironic.

'And Nell for saving the day.'

'Congratulations, by the way.' He reached for an

umbrella from behind the office door. 'I wondered if she wouldn't do that.'

Camryn stopped dead in the middle of the room. 'What do you mean?'

'I told you to be patient, Camryn, and not to rush into anything—that there was time.'

'You knew that she had money?'

'I suspected it. And no, I wasn't snooping through her private files, just sorting out her mail. Most elderly people on pensions don't get letters from trust companies in New York and cable television franchises in Colorado and petroleum companies in Texas, all in the same day. Nell does.'

Her eyes narrowed. 'You manipulated me, and Nell, too?'

'No. I just dumped the ingredients together and waited to see what would happen. I couldn't honestly send you to another bank—the odds were no better for you there. And I couldn't ethically suggest that you ask Nell for help. But I could provide the opportunity. The rest was up to the two of you.' He sounded as if it didn't matter to him how it had turned out.

But he made it possible for me to keep my house, Camryn thought. Then he really didn't mean to force me to give it up, after all. . .

In the lobby they ran into Warren Stanford, who looked Camryn over speculatively and then asked Patrick, 'Shall I tell Dianna you'll stop by later? Now that she's feeling better, she'd like to see you, I know.'

Patrick didn't miss a step. 'I don't think so, Warren.'

So Dianna had been ill, Camryn thought.

By the time they reached the Stone House, the wind had picked up, and the rain was blowing in sheets.

Camryn had left her own car parked under the porte-cochère, so they had to run from the driveway to the front porch, and even with the umbrella, they all got thoroughly wet.

Patrick shook out the umbrella and looked doubtfully back across the drive. Susan was giggling and tugging at his hand. Camryn put her key in the lock and thought, I can't deal with a tantrum just now, and if he leaves she'll throw a king-sized one.

Oh, be honest, she told herself crossly. It isn't Susan I'm worried about, not really. Patrick's going to leave, and I'm the one who doesn't want to let him go——

'Come in and have some hot chocolate and wait out the storm,' she said. 'It has to stop some time.'

He hesitated, and for an instant Camryn felt as if the world itself hung in the balance. Then Susan said, 'Read me a story,' and he smiled at her.

He would have rather braved the rain, if it had been only me, Camryn thought wearily as she waited for the hot chocolate to come almost to a boil. But for Susan. . .

The solarium was quiet, except for the rhythm of the rain striking the windows, when she carried in the three big mugs, each topped with whipped cream and fragrant with cinnamon. She was startled by the silence until she saw Susan sound asleep on the couch, curled up under a blanket with her thumb in her mouth.

Patrick was standing by the window, arms folded across his chest, watching the storm. He had taken his jacket off, and his sleeves were rolled to the elbow. He turned at the click of the tray against the glass table and came quickly across the room. 'She only lasted through a story and a half,' he said. 'I just straightened her out and covered her.'

She handed him a mug. 'She gets so tired that when

she slows down for anything, a nap attacks her.' She picked up his tie from the back of a chair; the silk was rain-spotted. 'Your cleaning bills must have gone through the roof since you met us.'

He smiled a little. 'It's all right, Camryn. You don't have to try so hard. I think it would be better if I just left.' He set his mug back on the tray.

She took a sip, and didn't care that the liquid scalded her tongue; at least that was a good excuse for the tears that stung her eyes. 'Susan won't be very happy if you aren't here when she wakes up.'

'The world doesn't revolve around Susan.' It was almost harsh. He reached for his tie and started to knot it briskly.

'Are you going to see Dianna after all?' That, she thought, must be the dumbest question I've ever asked. You've got no dignity left, Camryn Hastings——

'Does it matter?'

And why should you be worried about dignity? she asked herself. It hasn't gotten you anywhere, that's for sure. Maybe it's time to try honesty instead. . .'Yes, it matters.' It was only a whisper, but his hands stopped in mid-motion. She swallowed hard, but something in his eyes forced her on. 'It matters a great deal, Patrick.'

He looked down at her for a long moment, and then very deliberately he took the cup from her hand and set it aside and pulled her almost roughly into his arms. There was desperation in his kiss and raw hunger in the way she responded to him, as if they would never again be so close, never again share this marvellous reality. . .

Then he let her go. 'I shouldn't have done that,' he said, and finished knotting his tie with hands that trembled a little.

Camryn felt as cold as if she had been snatched up in

the middle of a dream and dumped into cold water. 'Why not?' she said crisply. 'Because I might get the wrong ideas?'

'I can't think how you could, Camryn. I made myself very plain, and I'm not going to apologise for it.' He half turned to face her, and his voice was deliberate. 'Even though I would give anything to be able to say I didn't mean a word of it, I can't. It's too important to me——'

'What you said about Mitch?' she whispered.

'I'm not backing down from that, Camryn. No man can compete with a saint, and I'm not going to try!'

Her throat was tight. 'I'm not asking you to,' she said. 'Patrick, you were right. I have been giving Mitch credit for too many things, and remembering only what I wanted to. . .'

The uncertainty in his face hurt her. 'That's easy enough to say now,' he said bitterly. 'Now that his memorial is safe.' He flung out a hand in a gesture that encompassed the room, and everything beyond.

'The house?' she whispered. 'Is that what you think? That I'm so determined to keep it because it stands for Mitch?'

The Stone House isn't big enough for you and me and Mitch,' he had said.

'If you really hate the house——' she began uncertainly, and stopped. What could she offer him—a promise to sell it? But that would mean giving up her business, and her independence. . .

'It's not the house. It's just what it stands for.'

'But it doesn't, Patrick. It was never really Mitch's house. He wanted a new one in the suburbs. I wanted lots of space and good, old construction. He finally said it was up to me—I was the one who would spend all my time here.'

'Camryn——' He sounded as if he'd been hit squarely in the solar plexus.

She went on, unhearing. 'He was right. He was home a couple of nights a week—one day, maybe. Sometimes not even that. I told myself that it was necessary, and that he was helping people. I tried not to mind. I would have exploded eventually, I suppose, but he died instead, and so I just kept hiding from the truth, until you forced me to take a good look at myself.'

He said, uncomfortably, 'I'm sorry, Camryn.'

'Don't stop me. I have to do this—I've held it in too long.' She took a deep breath. 'I didn't want him to go on that last trip. I hoped he'd stay at home, with Susan and me. We'd scarcely seen him in weeks, and she was growing so fast. He didn't even know she could pull herself up to the furniture—he never knew. After he died, I guess I just wanted to prove that I could hold things together—that my love for him hadn't been in vain——'

'Camryn——'

'I couldn't keep on being what he wanted, Patrick. But I can't wipe him out of my memory completely. Whether you like it or not, he was a part of my life. He wasn't a saint, but he wasn't a villain, either!'

There was a long silence, and then he said, very quietly, 'I know. And I'm not asking you to forget about him altogether.'

She turned uncertainly. 'You're not?'

He shook his head. 'No—because that's part of you, Camryn, part of the woman I love. Just remember him as he really was, that's all I ask.' He held out his arms, and she found herself huddling against him as if she had been freezing.

'Because,' he went on softly, 'I'm morally certain that

some time in the next fifty years I'm going to fall off the pedestal you've put me on——'

She shook her head. 'You're not on a pedestal. I thought from the first minute I met you that you were irritating, annoying, bossy——'

'See why I can't compete with a saint?' His smile had an ironic twist.

'You didn't like me much that day, either.' But her voice was muffled against his shoulder. This, she thought, is where I will always belong.

Patrick shook his head. 'No, I didn't. But it's not like me to judge people so quickly. It was only later that I realised it wasn't you I disliked at all—it was that damned wedding ring you were wearing like armour.' His hands cupped her face and turned it up to his. 'Will you wear mine instead? Will you marry me?'

'What about the Stone House, Patrick?'

'Run it if you like, give it up if you like. I wasn't trying to order you around by asking you to give up the restaurant; I was just trying to make sure there was time for me.' His voice was soft. 'My idea of a marriage is a partnership, Camryn—a bargain between equals. There isn't room in that for telling each other what to do, just for sharing hopes and dreams and problems.'

She hesitated. 'And memories? What about the memories we don't share, Patrick?'

'As long as we face them honestly, we'll be stronger for them. Camryn, you'll have to be patient with me. I *am* jealous of Mitch—of all the things you shared with him. But I'm not afraid of him any more.'

There was no denying the husky honesty in his voice. Tears stung her eyes. Afraid of Mitch? Yes, she could see that now. And she could understand why he had felt that way.

'I love you,' she whispered.

It was a much different sort of kiss, tender and satisfying and yet with the promise of all the world to come. . .

A long time later, Camryn said, still just a bit breathless, 'And you don't have to be jealous of Mitch—that's all past. Just as Dianna is.'

'Who?' She was sitting on his lap by then, and he was tracing her profile with kisses. He sounded abstracted.

'You heard me. You had tea with her last week, remember? You must have had some reason to put yourself through that ordeal——'

He laughed. 'It was a very special occasion. Remember that night at the picnic when she and her friend wandered off into the bushes? Dianna spent the next week lying in a darkened room, nursing a full-blown case of poison ivy. Warren asked me to drop by to cheer her up, and she threw me out when I asked how she'd managed to get it in so many interesting places.'

Camryn gave a little gurgle of laughter.

'I think she's finally given up the idea of wanting to marry me. I'm just too hopelessly middle class, I guess,' he murmured. 'I'd much rather sit on a park bench and eat cheeseburgers with you than have snails at the Ritz with Dianna.' He put his cheek down against her hair. 'And I'd rather admire chalk drawings on my own front path than works of art at the Louvre, too. Which reminds me—about Susan. . .'

'Thank heaven for Susan. If it hadn't been for her, you'd have been gone today.'

He shook his head. 'Not permanently. I was going to see you and try again, even if I had to batter the front door in. I didn't plan to use Susan, either; it wouldn't have been fair to her.' He sighed. 'Camryn, I swear I'm not doing this to try to wipe Mitch out of your life and Susan's, but would you think about letting me adopt her? I don't want her to be the odd child, you see—the one with the different name. I want to really be her father.'

'There are going to be more children?' she asked demurely. But there was a catch in her breath; she wasn't sure if it was from the idea of another generation of McKennas—dark-haired, blue-eyed, strong-willed and thoroughly charming—or the ravishing touch of Patrick's hands against her breasts. She answered her own question. 'I wouldn't be surprised if there are several.'

He smiled, but his voice was serious. 'And will you think about Susan?'

She shook her head. 'I don't have to, Patrick. I couldn't ask for a better father for her.'

'You won't regret it, I promise you. Will you marry me soon?'

His lips were trailing down her throat, and his thumb was drawing sensual circles over her nipple.

'I think I'd better, don't you?' She was a little breathless.

'Well, I could keep this up until you give in.'

'In that case, Patrick, I might need a week or two to think about it.'

He laughed. 'And Nell told me a young woman in love wasn't capable of being rational!'

'That's funny. She told me the same thing about you.' She put her head down on his shoulder. 'Shall we call her up and tell her that we came to our senses?'

'Later,' Patrick murmured. 'After all, she's the one who's got all the patience in the world.'

HARLEQUIN
Romance®

Coming Next Month

Available in September wherever paperback books are sold, or
through Harlequin Reader Service:

In the U.S.
901 Fuhrmann Blvd.
P.O. Box 1397
Buffalo, N.Y. 14240-1397

In Canada
P.O. Box 603
Fort Erie, Ontario
L2A 5X3

HARLEQUIN
American Romance®

THE LOVES OF A CENTURY...

Join American Romance in a nostalgic look back at the Twentieth Century—at the lives and loves of American men and women from the turn-of-the-century to the dawn of the year 2000.

Journey through the decades from the dance halls of the 1900s to the discos of the seventies ... from Glenn Miller to the Beatles ... from Valentino to Newman ... from corset to miniskirt ... from beau to Significant Other.

Relive the moments ... recapture the memories.

Look now for the CENTURY OF AMERICAN ROMANCE series in Harlequin American Romance. In one of the four American Romance titles appearing each month, for the next twelve months, we'll take you back to a decade of the Twentieth Century, where you'll relive the years and rekindle the romance of days gone by.

Don't miss a day of the CENTURY OF AMERICAN ROMANCE.

A CENTURY OF
AMERICAN ROMANCE
1900's

The women...the men...the passions...
the memories....

CAR-1

Harlequin Superromance®

THE LIVING WEST

Where men and women must be strong in both body
and spirit; where the lessons of the past must be fully
absorbed before the present can be understood; where
the dramas of everyday lives are played out against a
panoramic setting of sun, red earth, mountain and
endless sky....

Harlequin Superromance is proud to present this
powerful new trilogy by Suzanne Ellison, a veteran
Superromance writer who has long possessed a
passion for the West. Meet Joe Henderson, whose past
haunts him—and his romance with Mandy Larkin;
Tess Hamilton, who isn't sure she can make a life with
modern-day pioneer Brady Trent, though she loves
him desperately; and Clay Gann, who thinks the
cultured Roberta Wheeler isn't quite woman enough
to make it in the rugged West....

Please join us for HEART OF THE WEST (September
1990), SOUL OF THE WEST (October 1990) and
SPIRIT OF THE WEST (November 1990) and see the
West come alive!

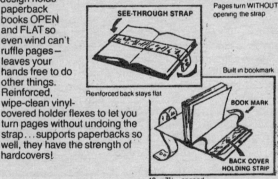